The Wise & Foolish Tongue

CELTIC STORIES

& POEMS

Collected and Told by Robin Williamson

CHRONICLE BOOKS • SAN FRANCISCO

First published in the United States in 1991 by Chronicle Books.

First published in Great Britain in 1989 by Canongate Publishing, Ltd.

Printed in the United States of America

Williamson, Robin, 1943–
[Craneskin bag]
The wise and foolish tongue: Celtic stories and poems / collected
and told by Robin Williamson.
p.   cm.
Reprint. Originally published: The craneskin bag. Edinburgh:
Canongate, 1989.
Includes bibliographical references.
ISBN 0-87701-867-7
1. Celts–Great Britain–Literary collections.   2. Celtic
literature–Adaptations.   I. Title.
PR6073.I433413C7   1991
828′.91409-dc20   90-49663
CIP

Distributed in Canada by Raincoast Books,
112 East Third Avenue, Vancouver, B.C. V5T 1C8

10   9   8   7   6   5   4   3   2   1

Chronicle Books
275 Fifth Street
San Francisco, CA 94103

to my wife Bina and my son Gavin

CONTENTS

vi

THE WISE AND FOOLISH TONGUE

HEROES AND DESTINY

vii

FOREWORD

Traditional story-telling has enjoyed over the last few years a gentle reawakening as a branch of the performing arts, a revival in which I've had the privilege to be a part. I doubt that any Scot can grow up entirely immune to the legends of his country, and for me the folklore, songs and music of Scotland and the rest of Britain and Ireland have always been an important key to my own work. But because I am by trade a poet who makes music and a musician who writes books, I have always drawn not only on the oral but also on the written heritage; particularly the literature of ancient Britain, the early Welsh literature. Much of this relates to the part of the country which is now the Scottish Borders, my own origins, either because of its authors' provenance in ancient Northern kingdoms (before the seventh century AD, the northern limit of the Welsh speaking kingdoms was central Scotland) or because the stories appear to be set there. Arthurian legends, for instance, are quite often northerly in their setting.

The Celtic classics have an extraordinarily vivid and present flavour, yet have been all too often unavailable, scarce, or forbiddingly scholarly in English versions. On the other hand, elements of Celtic lore have been loosely adapted to the fields of fantasy, sword and sorcery, and romantic novels, without due credit or fidelity to the sources. My concern throughout has been to render the early Welsh and Irish bardic material as living poetry. I have endeavoured to convey the spirit, word-music, and vigour of the originals as well as their sense, and to convey the stories with characteristic tricks, mannerisms and personal elaboration of the traditional heritage. I have been intrigued and delighted to observe the more ancient material finding a new place for itself among English speakers alongside the current folk tradition. In short, my renderings of these pieces are not offered so much as versions of manuscript originals or as literal translations, but as developed in my performances throughout the world. Basically, I feel that as a travelling story-teller and harper, I have acquired insight into them that could have been acquired in no other way.

I became particularly involved with the ancient Welsh legends, for instance, during the presentation of the *Mabinogion* by Moving Being Theatre company at Caernarfon and Cardiff castles in 1983; I composed the music for this production which was televised by Channel Four in Britain. Subsequent theatre productions drew on the Arthurian and early Merlin cycles, and various deeper meanings of all this material became increasingly apparent to me.

Thus perhaps the most important ingredient in my selection of pieces for this book has been the interplay between performer and audience.

It was the custom of the earliest Celtic story-tellers to categorise their material under certain headings: elopements, cattle raids, battles, feasts, visions and so on. I have grouped the pieces here in the same way, according to their subject matter, and regardless of place of origin or period.

The most common motifs in Celtic folktale feature voyages to the other world, a fool who succeeds, tasks done for love, and so on. One does not encounter stories intended to explain the basis of existence, or dealing with the deeds of animals before the time of humans. One finds no explanations of the sun, the moon, lightning or fire. No trace of a creation myth. One wonders if such a myth has been lost since Christian times, or was it that the ancient Celts believed the universe to have been without beginning, always present? They seem to have believed in personal reincarnation. More than one Roman author mentions the lending of money among the Celts on which repayment was to be made in a future lifetime. But perhaps the primary Celtic beliefs are in the power of enchantment. Magic is native to Celtic literature. Not even the earliest hero tales are without the presence of wizardry or occult skills.

Warriors are often wizards, wizards are often poets.

The names in the old stories were of great importance, and were used by the old poets for strong evocative power. Therefore, in print, I have opted for the look of the ancient spellings of names where appropriate, as well as supplying phonetic versions.

The Celts attributed to their poets, the bards, a sacred status as the conveyers of praise (which confirmed a ruler in his strength, a hero in his fame), or satire (which made laughing-stocks of the highest, could make mad, or kill). Bards were mentioned as a branch of the Druid order about the first century AD by the Roman author Strabo, who also distinguished between bards and eubates. Bards, broadly speaking, were concerned with verse and song for harp, eubates were students of philosophy. Strabo also stated, 'Poetry is the first philosophy that ever was taught'. Bards continued as the advisers and confidants of Celtic nobility throughout the Middle Ages and to a lesser extent and in a debased form even into the eighteenth century.

Druids (the priestly class of the Celtic people) had such power that if they crossed a field of battle the combatants would cease fighting and let them pass. Similar to the Druids, the *filid* of Ireland were the repository of the tales which portray the curious tangle of honour, guile, wisdom, and cruelty which appear to have constituted Celtic notions of Deity. Regrettably, all the earliest philosophic or religious material of Britain and Ireland, being oral rather than written, is unrecoverable. The Druids were not in the habit of discussing it with Roman or other invaders, or anyone not initiated into their order. So apart from fragmentary material which remains in folk tradition and the very few surviving literary treasures, such as 'The Spoils of Annwn' and 'The Battle of the Trees', which hint at their Druid origins or antecedents, a large proportion of early bardic poetry remaining to us takes the form of eulogy of patrons or elegy of the heroic dead. But wonderful and really ancient stories remain. They have been described as a window on the Iron Age. Presumably certain blatantly pagan elements were excised by the church scribes, in whose manuscripts alone this material was recorded. But it is surprising what a wealth has survived.

And I hope the pieces in this collection will work their magic on you as they have on me, and that they will serve as an entertaining introduction to the intricate beauty of the Celtic mind.

I

A CALENDAR OF JOURNEYS

There is an interplay between this world and the 'otherworld', shown in the ruler's close relationship to the health and well-being of his land. A special magical relationship exists between the ruler and the year. And central to this motif is the idea that women may personify aspects of deity.

THE WOOING OF ISOLDE

IF YOU WERE TO STROLL ROUND DUBLIN'S FAIR CITY, SMILING
at nothing in particular or watching the big mullet slapping
through the Liffey's grimy shallows, or smelling the coffee
roasting in Bewley's, or listening to what the pigeons and
the preacher have to say to each other on Stephen's Green,
you wouldn't be wasting your time, to my way of thinking.
But if you began reading the destinations on the buses
you'd eventually see one for Chapelizod. And there's a story
in that. Not many remember now that Chapelizod is named
after Isolde, the beautiful Isolde, Isolde of the White Throat,
long ago daughter to the King of Dublin.

She was to be married to March son of Meirchion[1]
King of Cornwall. Arthur High King of the Britons sent
March's kinsman Tristan over to Ireland to fetch the lady
to her wedding.

Tristan was a great harper, but like many a bard of
those days he was also a warrior. And he had magical
skills. For while his music could charm the birds from the
bushes, he had other power. If anyone would wound him,
that one would die. And if he would wound anyone, that
one would die. So conveying the most beautiful lady of the
western world across hills of brigands, through forests full
of heraldic beasts and over a sea awash with lonely pirates
was no particular trouble to him.

It was on a sultry day they sailed away from Dublin—
the sea like a millpond. The sails hung limp. The oars were
out. The rowers were sweating at them and cursing the
weather quietly and thoroughly. Tristan and Isolde sat
together in the bows. He played the harp to her a while.
They played chess a while. And after a while, being thirsty,
they sent a page below for some refreshment.

But, the first bottle the page put his hand upon was
the flask of love potion made for Isolde by her father's
wizard, to be drunk only as directed between Isolde and
March at their wedding. The page brought up a couple of

half-gills of it, Tristan and Isolde each took a sip, and fell at once and forever in love.

As this fact fully dawned on them, they stared horror-stricken, each with arms outstretched to the other, for how could their love ever be, since Isolde was promised to March? And Tristan, being a man of honour, under oath, insisted on delivering Isolde to King March as promised.

So there was Isolde in March's castle, refusing to speak or eat and Tristan stalking the wilds of Albion, seeking to ease his grief in quest, combat, dragon slaying and such.

Finally this life of stolen glimpses, servants' messages, and midnight assignations proved unbearable. The lovers eloped together to the Forest of Caledon, that cloaked old Scotland from Forth to Clyde and from Berwick to Galloway, the wildest and deepest woods in all the lands of Arthur.

Now messengers were sent to Arthur from the enraged King March, who demanded justice. And Arthur sent for his wisest councillors and debated long on this. For Tristan could not be brought back by force, and March would not be propitiated with gold.

When he had taken full counsel, Arthur set off for Caledon with King March and his retinue. Arriving there, the finest poets and harpers were sent forward, through the groves, to Tristan. These he would never harm. And the poets and harpers presented the King's words so well that Tristan and Isolde came willingly to Arthur and agreed to abide by his judgement, whatever it might be.

Arthur decreed that Isolde should spend the half year when the trees were in leaf with one man, and the half year when the trees were bare with the other. King March was to have the first choice, as the injured party.

March thought to himself, 'In winter the nights are longer, and the days seem longer,' and he said: 'I will have Isolde when the trees are bare.'

At that, Isolde laughed aloud and clapped her hands and she said:

'Blessed be the judgement
blessed the tongue that utters it
and blessed the pen that records it
three trees there are, loyal and true
the holly, the ivy and the yew
that keep their leaves all year through'

So Tristan was wed to Isolde, and so this story ends. Some say Chapelizod is where she was buried years later in Dublin. Some say a little ruined chapel stood there till Victorian times, a little Christian chapel on an ancient site. At all events, it's under a building site now. As for King March's castle, well, the ruins of that are parts of a farm that stands in Cornwall to this day. But where Tristan's grave might be, or what became of his wonderful music, no one knows.

of early Celtic origin;
first texts c. 1550

KING BRAN AND THE LAND OF
MANANNÁN MAC LIR

THE OTHERWORLD OF THE CELTIC PEOPLES HAS ALWAYS
been perceived as ever present beside our own. Sometimes
under the sea, or a loch, or within a hill, or far to the west.
It was the land of the immortals, and the heroes, and might
on occasion be visited by the people of the earth, especially
by poets. Tír na n-Óg it is called, Land of the Young, and
Land of the Living, and Land of Women and many another
name. It has been said that there are certain places on this
world very close to the other where the two worlds meet.
Sometimes a voyage is necessary, as in this ancient Irish
story of Bran, son of Febal.[1]

One day, Bran son of Febal was walking near his royal hall
when an air of sweet music lulled him from his senses.
When he awoke there was a branch of silver by him, with
white blossoms on it. He took it home with him, and later,
when all were assembled, a beautiful woman appeared in
their midst arrayed in raiment rich and strange. These are
the words she spoke, as the bards relate:

>   horses out of the bright sea
>   course ever about my own land
>   that is borne by four noble columns
>   where the waves and the deep sky are joined
>
>   white of day on the brave reward
>   plain of the sea where hosts contend
>   battle bouts of boats and chariots
>   in the fine plain south of the silver land
>
>   columns of white bronze beneath her
>   delight and light of numbered worlds
>   home of kindness beyond life's gulf
>   where blossom blooms and flowers flower

Febal (Fay vil)

there is a tree of flowers
there perch the birds of melody[2]
calling together each changed hour
with perfect and habitual harmony

hues of every tint tuned
enchanting chant of women singers
habitual joy to harp sound
in the plain south of the cloud of silver

there is no grief or treason
there is the favoured haunt of pleasure
no taunt, threat, or malediction
but sweet of music strikes the ear

there is no sorrow, death or mourning
health and strength unweakening
are in the nature of that haven
wonder without comparison

there is beauty underfoot
gracefulness in all appearance
there is beauty on all sides
over all a mist of sweetness

sight yearns for the plain of kindness
pebbled with dragon stone and glass
where curling waves are about her shores
combing sea clear crystal tresses

there is every colour of riches
freshness there in full abound
there is heard the tune of softness
there is drinking of the finest wine

chariots of gold in the plain of the sea
come with the waves towards the sun
chariots of silver in the plain of games
faultless chariots of bronze

horses of yellow gold on the beaches
horses the purple of royalty
horses upon the shoulders of the ocean
as blue a blue as the blue sky

there comes with the dawn of day
the pure man by whom light is shed
who runs the white plain that strikes the sea
stirs up the sea till it seems blood

land of guises before the sea
seeming near seeming far
many fine women of every beauty
the pure sea encircles there

the while sweet chords of music sound
birds sing in the height of peace
a chorus of women from the high land
descend towards the plain contests

happiness with health endowed
in the land where laughter rises
in the width and depth of peace
endlessness of royal riches

endlessness of gentle weather
silverly scattered over all
where white rock and white sea shine together
where the warmth of sunlight falls

music is heard out of the darkness
a journey ends where colours crowd
splendour is on a crown there
and from it shines a white cloud

The lady urged Bran to make ready a ship to sail to the
west, for at this time he would be able to reach the land of
joy. And she said:

not to every man is my offer made
though every man may hear the words
let you, Bran, among the many
understand what you have heard

So Bran made ready a fine ship and with certain chosen
companions set sail for the west. And as they were sailing,
after two days and two nights, they met Manannán mac
Lir, the Son of the Sea driving his two wheeled chariot over
the waves. And Manannán spoke these words then:

King Bran in your vessel steering
you think you are sailing over the billows
I in my chariot of long faring
behold you rowing over a meadow

where you pull over ocean clear
King Bran with your skiff of rowers
I in my two wheeled chariot steer
across a wide plain of flowers

King Bran with keen regard
scans the waves that slap and skirmish
I myself see green sward
and red beaked flowers without blemish

sea waves like the spines of mares
as far as King Bran's eyes can peer
rivers pour honey in showers
in the land of Manannán mac Lir

the sea you see you see as blue
you see white waves where you are rowing
finest fields of verdant hue
under my wheels where I am going

out of the womb of the combing sea
speckled salmon leap from the water
they are my calves, my coloured lambs
unknown to them is man's murder

9

King Bran sees one chariot rider
prancing over plain or ocean
countless steeds are on its surface
though your eyes cannot see them

full of disport, full of pleasure
rejoicing in the wine of vigour
among green bushes without sin
men and women are lying together

your boat scrapes among hill peaks
among the boughs of lofty oaks
orchards of the right fruit
are under the bow of your little boat

trees in blossom and fruit at once
breathe the breath of the true vine
trees with neither blight nor fault
gold leaves on their branches shine

we are since time awoke
without age or the grave's oppression
we do not wait to be old and weak
by no sin are we overtaken

The Son of the Sea directed Bran on his way so that he did come to the Land of Joy, and to the Land of Women. But after a certain time, one of Bran's company became deeply homesick, so they sailed to see how Ireland fared. Crowds of people flocked to the quay where they were coming in. Yet when Bran addressed them, none knew of Bran son of Febal, save as a name from an ancient story. The homesick man leapt ashore, but as soon as his feet touched the earth of Erin he crumbled into the dust of ages. Bran ordered that an account of the voyage they had made should be set down by the writers of Ireland. And so it was, in the seventh century after Christ. Then, without ever disembarking, Bran and his men sailed away again into the sea and from that hour their wanderings are not known.

Original manuscript: eight-century Irish,
Immram Brain, *Voyage of Bran*

GOGMAGOG AND THE FIRST KINGS OF BRITAIN

ACCORDING TO THE TWELFTH — CENTURY CLERIC GEOFFREY of Monmouth, the primal name of Britain was Albion,[1] a green and pleasant land, watered with rivers full of fish and endowed with forests full of game. In ancient times a small number of giants were the only inhabitants. But into this land came, after the fall of Troy, Brutus the Trojan and his companions. They landed at the port of Totnes[2] and established themselves in certain districts, driving the dispossessed giants before them into remote fastnesses where they took refuge in caves.

Now Brutus named the island after himself, and hence it is called Britain to this day. And the language spoken there, once called Trojan or crooked Greek, is now called British. The country being divided by lot among Brutus and his kinsmen, the southern part fell to one Corineus and he named it Cornwall, after his own name. Corineus wished to rule this part above all others, for he loved to fight with giants and Cornwall was a great stronghold of these.

It was there lived Gogmagog,[3] twelve cubits in height, whose favoured weapon was an oak tree he would uproot and wield as a club. Gogmagog slaughtered many of the invaders of his country, but at length he was captured and set to wrestle with Corineus.

Gogmagog took a hold on Corineus, which cracked three ribs on the man. Then Corineus took a hold on Gogmagog, heaved him over his head and over a cliff and to his death on the rocks of the sea below.

Well the royal descendants of Brutus increased and multiplied. Though one Mempricius not only murdered his brother, but preferred unnatural intercourse to natural love and was devoured by wolves for his sins. His son Ebraucus, legendary founder of Edinburgh, then called Mount Agned or Painted Mountain, and later the City of Maidens[4] or the Mount Dolorous, is said to have begotten twenty sons by twenty wives and thirty daughters he begat also.

From these fertile loins descends Bladud, who is said to have cured himself of leprosy and founded on the site of this cure the town of Bath. He was one of the first British aviators and met thereby his death, for the pair of wings he had made himself broke in full flight and he crashed on Ludgate Hill where now St Paul's Cathedral stands.

And the other great early British flyer was Abaris, who travelled through the air to Greece by means of a sort of golden arrow. And it is said that either Abaris or Bladud, but certainly one or the other was the instructor of Pythagoras.

And Bladud was father to the man we call King Lear, whose sad story Shakespeare adjusted to his own uses. But among the Welsh there was the more ancient story of the one they call Lludd,[5] or Nudd, and of his daughter, 'the most splendid maiden in the three islands of Britain or the three islands adjacent'. Her name was Creiddylad.[6]

She had two suitors, named Gwyn ap Nudd[7] and Gwythyr ap Greidyawl.[8] Each was in turn stealing Creiddylad away from the other.

Now these were all immortals. Gwyn ap Nudd was the lord of the hosts of the dead and of shadows, and Gwythyr ap Greidyawl, if his name is anything to go by (Conqueror, son of Burning Heat) was of the solar-deity class. For centuries the dispute raged between Gwyn and Gwythyr. Finally, it was resolved by Arthur, who decreed that the two should fight for Creiddylad every first of May[9] until the Day of Doom. And whoever by then was victorious would win the maiden.

original text: Geoffrey of Monmouth,
Historia Regum Brittaniae (*History of the Kings of Britain*)
1136

Lludd (thleethe)   Creiddylad (cray thúl ad)   Nudd (neethe)
Gwythyr ap Greidyawl (gwi theer ap gry dowel)

THE MONTH OF MAY

May it is
fair faced and gentle
blackbirds exult at the crack of day

cuckoos' work greets lordly summer
a balm it is for every bitterness
hedge-green bristle the branching boughs

summer shallows
thirsty herds hasten there
heather's hair sprouts
bog cotton flourishes

tides of smoothness
the ocean drowses
flowers decorate the world

bees bear their weight of harvest
high hills call the cows
the ant feasts

harp of the trees hums and soothes
colour reposes on each slope
haze upon the brimming lake

the corn-crake croaks on, merciless poet
pure falls fall to the warm pool
rushes regain their voice of whispers
swallows soar and dart above

ardent music rings the hill
fruit of sweetness is in the bud
the dusty cuckoo cries and calls

speckled fish are at their leaping
strength is on the swift hero
strength of man is in full flower
majesty of heights unmarred
fair are the woods from root to twig

fair each fresh and fertile field
ever pleasant the garb of spring
winter gales past and gone

cheerfulness on every good grove
restful, happy, sunlit time
flutterings of birds flock down
green fields full of answerings
where the busy water sparkles

a passion sparks for the racing of horses
where warriors are arrayed
rich verges of the cattle pool
lend gold to the iris flower

shy unyielding lark
the burden of your song is clear
bonny serene May is perfect

Irish, author unknown; c. ninth century

CULHWCH AND OLWEN

The story of Isolde and the earlier story of Creiddylad have seasonal significance, but of all such stories Culhwch and Olwen is the greatest. Quirky humour, gory detail, impossible feats and magic abound in this quest, part myth part folktale from ancient Wales. I expect a good story-teller in the old days could spin this one out for a whole winter if the hospitality was forthcoming. Culhwch and Olwen is in the *Mabinogion* and is one of the earliest stories in which Arthur features.

The mother of Culhwch, a beautiful but temperamental lady, became unsettled in her wits during her pregnancy, strayed from civilised places and, returning to her senses near her time, found herself amongst a herd of pigs. She gave birth to her son in fright at that. The swineherd took the boy to court. That's how Culhwch got his name. It means Pig Run. But he was a king's son, and a cousin to Arthur himself. He was fostered, as was the custom, to a high-born family.

His mother, Goleuddydd,[1] now become mortally ill. She required her royal husband to promise that he would never marry again until he would see a two-headed briar growing on her grave. Secretly, she had requested her old teacher to trim the grave to the ground every year. Goleuddydd died. The king went every morning to look at her grave to see if anything was growing there. At the end of the seventh year, Goleuddydd's old teacher forgot to trim the grave. In the spring thereafter, the king found a briar growing and asked his counsellors to advise him in the choice of a new wife.

'How about the wife of King Doged?' was the word he was given. So they made war on King Doged, killed him and carried his widow and daughter back with them. They took possession of King Doged's land also, very good land it was.

Culhwch (kil hooch)   Goleuddydd (gol éy thith)

Now Doged's royal widow was nothing if not adaptable. What seemed to bother her most was that the man who had carried her off so vigorously appeared to have no children. Finally she inquired privily of an old woman concerning this, saying: 'Sad it is to be wedded to an infertile man.'

'Neither stars nor portents deny him children,' said the hag. 'He shall have children, and by you, I prophesy, my lady, God bless your generosity. Grieve no longer, God reward you, for he has one son.'

That night the lady asked her husband why he had concealed his son from her. 'I will conceal him from you no longer,' said the king. He sent messengers to bring Culhwch back to court.

At a quiet moment soon after, Culhwch's stepmother suggested to him that her daughter would make a wonderful wife for any nobleman.

'I do not wish to marry yet,' said Culhwch.

'I put a curse on you then,' said his stepmother. 'Your flesh shall never touch the flesh of a woman till you get Olwen daughter of Ysbaddaden King of all Giants.'

Culhwch blushed at that. Passionate love and desire for Olwen possessed him, though he had never seen her. He blushed often thereafter. One day his father asked him why.

'My stepmother has put a curse on me that my flesh will never touch the flesh of a woman till I get Olwen daughter of Ysbaddaden King of all Giants.'

'That's easy for you to achieve, my son. Go to King Arthur, your cousin. Ask him to trim your hair,[2] as a cousinly act of affection, and while he is about it ask that he accomplish this quest for you. He will not fail you.'

Culhwch rode off on a young grey steed
of fiery eye, of graceful pace
gold, not leather, about its head

Ysbaddaden (us bath áhden)

gold, not leather, its saddle was
and Culhwch bore two silver spears
his sword in hand an arm's length
it would wound the wind and swifter drop
than drops the wettest dew of June
on Culhwch's hip, gold hilted
a gold edged sword with a gold cross on it
many jewelled as the midnight sky
moon white its ivory grip
by Culhwch there ran two dappled hounds
red gold collars from shoulder to ear
the dog on the left would leap to the right
the dog on the right would leap to the left
like two wild birds they sported round him
the four hooves of Culhwch's steed
would hurl four clods above Culhwch's head
like four of summer's swooping swallows
a purple, four-cornered cloak he wore
a red gold apple at every corner
each apple worth a hundred cows
the gold in his soft boots and lacings
from the knob of his knee to the nail of his toe
three hundred cows would hardly buy
so easily the steed moved under him
no curl of Culhwch's hair was stirred
nor even the least tip of one hair
so Culhwch came riding to Arthur's gate

'Is there a gate-keeper?'

'There is, and may you not keep your head on your shoulders for asking such a question,' came the churlish reply from behind closed doors. 'I am gate-keeper to Arthur every first of January and my subordinates for the rest of the year are Huandaw, Gogigwr, Llaesgenym and Penpingion, who hops on his head to save his feet, never standing nor lying down, but like a rolling stone on the floor of Arthur's court.'

Gogigwr (gog íg oor)   Llaesgenym (thlice gén im)

'Open the gate,' said Culhwch.

'I will not,' said the gate-keeper.

'Why will you not?' said Culhwch.

'Knife has gone into meat, drink into drinking horn, there is already a great crowd in the court of Arthur. No one may enter but the son of a king or a man of skill who comes with his craft. You'll get food for your dogs, grain for your horse. You'll get peppered chops and brimming beakers of wine. You'll get enough for fifty in the hostel down the road where strangers who have no right to insist on Arthur's hospitality are accommodated. You'll be just as well off there as Arthur is in his own court, I assure you. You'll get songs to entertain you and a woman to sleep with you, and tomorrow when the gates are opened to permit the exit of the thronging crowds who have descended on us today, they shall be opened to you first of all. And tomorrow, you can seat yourself anywhere you may choose in Arthur's hall.'

'None of this will do,' said Culhwch. 'If you open the door now, well and good. If not, I will voice an ill report of your lord and yourself throughout the land. Further, I will shout three shouts at this gate that will be heard as clearly southerly on the moors of Cornwall, northerly on the shores of the Scots north and on the Accursed Ridge[3] in Ireland. All pregnant women in the court will miscarry, and all other women here, from the time they hear these shouts, will never conceive at all.'

'Whatever uproar you may raise for the privileges of Arthur's court, you shall not enter,' said the gate-keeper adding hastily, 'Not until I speak to Arthur first.'

The gate-keeper Glewlwyd[4] strode off and flung open the door of Arthur's feasting hall. 'What news from the gate?' asked the king in some surprise. Glewlwyd drew himself up to his full height and, in the grand manner of Taliesin, he proclaimed:

'Two parts of my life have gone
and two parts of your own

Glewlwyd (gleh loid)

I have been in Caer Se and Caer Asse
in Sach and Salach
in Lotor and Fotor
and Greater and Lesser India
I have been in the battle of the two Ynyrs[5]
when twelve hostages were taken from Llychlyn[6]
I have been once in Europe
I have been once in Africa, Corsica likewise
in Caer Brythwch and Brythach and Nerthach
I have been at hand when you killed the entire army
of Gleis[7] son of Merin
and when you killed Black Mil son of Dugum
I have been right beside you when you conquered Greece
   altogether
I have been, I declare, in Caer Oeth and Anoeth
the dark prisons under stone
and in Caer Nevenhyr of the nine natures'

'Yes, yes,' snapped Arthur, 'but what news from the gate?'

'Fair lords we encountered in performance of these exploits,' continued Glewlwyd, not a whit abashed, 'but I never saw a man as noble as he I have left standing at the gate in the rain.'

'If you came to me walking, go back running,' roared Arthur. 'Bring this man in. Servants, bring him a gold cup and keep it full. Give him some chops.'

It was the custom to dismount at the gate, but Culhwch, when the door was opened to him, rode straight into the hall dogs and all. 'Greetings, Lord of Kings in this island,' he said. 'May the low part of your house be no worse than the high. May this greeting reach equally your fighting men, your companions and your warlords. May no one here be deprived of this my greeting. May your fame, Arthur, resound throughout Britain.'

'Greetings to you also, chieftain. Sit here by me among the warriors. You shall have the privileges of a prince when you are here.'

Ynyrs (in eers)   Llychlyn (thlúhh lin)   Gleis (glayce)

'I did not come here for recognition, but to ask one boon of you.'

'You shall have whatever
your tongue can utter
while the wind blows with the wetness of rain
and the full extent
of your mind's invention
while sun lifts day to the last ebb of land
except my sword, my shield, my spear,
or my wife Gwenhwyfar.'[8]

'I ask first that my hair be trimmed.'

'You shall get that,' said Arthur, and taking a golden comb and silver handled scissors, he commenced to comb and trim the hair of Culhwch. But as he was about this he felt his heart warm to Culhwch, and he said to him, 'I know in my heart we must be kindred. Tell me who you are.'

'I will. I am Culhwch son of Cilydd son of Celyddon Wledig, and of Goleuddydd my mother.'

'Then,' said Arthur, 'you are my cousin. Claim what you will of me.'

'Help me to win the hand of Olwen daughter of Ysbaddaden King of all Giants.'

Culhwch invoked this help with a highly skilled bardic incantation on the names of Arthur's assembled warriors, not one of whom he had met before. He expanded with wit and delightful language upon their fame and prowess, till an hour was as a moment. And Culhwch invoked this help in the names of the greatest ladies of Arthur's court after Gwenhwyfar, with their full poetic titles, powers and beauties. And this incantation he performed with resonance, with good humour and with a melodious tongue.

'Well,' said Arthur finally. 'I never heard of Olwen or of this king of giants, but I will send messengers to seek news of her. It may take some time to find her.'

'I will give you from tonight until a year from

Gwenhwyfar (gwen hóy var)
Cilydd (Kilith)   Celyddon Wledig (Kel ithon wledig)

tomorrow night.'

At the end of a year, no news had been obtained. Culhwch became disgruntled and threatened to leave, reciting satires on Arthur's court throughout the island.

But Arthur's great warrior Cei[9] made this placation to him, saying: 'Do not be so hasty. Journey with us till you are satisfied that this maiden Olwen is not to be found in the world. Or until we find her.'

These were the powers of Cei:

> He could retain in sea deep
> one breath nine days and nights
> beyond herbs or healer's skill
> any wound he would inflict
> shadow light Cei could step
> or seem tree tall at will

Whatever Cei gripped would remain dry even in pelting rain from the heat of his hand, and in falling snow the snap of his fingers could kindle fire.

With them came Bedwyr[10] who never shied from any exploit in which Cei was engaged. He was the most beautiful man in Britain after Arthur and Drych[11] son of Cibddar.

> If he fought one-handed
> three armed men could not best him
> he gave with one spear thrust
> one death and nine defenses

With them went Cynddilyd the Guide, to whom all lands were as his own land, and Gwrhyr the Interpreter, to whom all tongues were as his own tongue and Gwalchmai,[12] who accomplished every quest he undertook and Menw,[13] who was a master of every kind of magic.

These heroes set forth upon their journey and they journeyed till they reached a huge plain, where grazed a flock of sheep as numerous as the white waves of the sea. And there, on a mound, sat a sheep dog as big as a cart

Cei (Kay)   Drych (drukh)   Cibddar (Kibthat)
Cynddilyd (kun thíl ig)   Gwrhyr (goor heer)   Menw (ménoo)

horse and a shepherd who was not undersized himself.

This was the shepherd's usual habit
to let no warrior pass unharmed
this was the strength of the shepherd's breath
to burn branches and brushwood down

'Go and speak to him,' said Cei to Gwrhyr. 'I only promised to go as far as you do,' said Gwrhyr to Cei. 'Fear not,' said Menw. 'I will put an enchantment on the dog so that he cannot harm us.' With some caution they went forward and gave the shepherd a most courteous greeting.

'How are you, noble shepherd?'

'Apart from my wife, no wound annoys me,' rumbled the shepherd.

'Whose sheep are these?'

'These are the sheep of Ysbaddaden King of all Giants. And whose sheep are you?'

'We are messengers from Arthur High King of Britain, sent to seek the hand of Olwen.' And they told him their names.

'More fools you,' laughed the shepherd, 'no cock upon that quest has ever lived to crow about it.'

Culhwch offered the shepherd, as a token of their good will, his gold armband, which the shepherd with a guffaw squeezed on to the little finger of his glove and, still laughing, strode off home to his wife.

'Where did you get that ring, husband?'

'Off a corpse the tide washed in.'

But the wife was not satisfied with such a reply, and she was not long in wheedling out the whole story. She knew then that Culhwch was her nephew, for she was the sister of Goleuddydd. And she determined to see him for herself.

As she ran joyfully towards these knights of Arthur with her arms outstretched to hug them, Cei, the first she came to grips with, had the presence of mind to snatch up a log between himself and her. And such was the ardour of her embrace that she made sap run from the log like whey from cheese. 'God knows,' muttered Cei:

'But for this log
that hug, you hag,
would have squeezed the last squawk
out of my bag'

Unoffendable, Culhwch's auntie invited them home for a meal. And after it, as they were conversing of this and that, she opened a cupboard by the fire and a beautiful yellow haired boy stepped out.

'What a pity to hide such a boy,' said Gwrhyr.

'The only one I have left,' said the shepherd's wife. 'Ysbaddaden has killed twenty-three of my sons, and my only hope is to keep this one out of his sight.'

'Let him remain with me,' said Cei. 'And he will not be slain unless I am. Help us to win Olwen for Culhwch your nephew.'

'For God's sake, venture no further with that. Ysbaddaden does not know you are here, go home while you can.'

But insisting they would not leave until they had seen the maiden, they at length found out that the shepherd's wife was Olwen's old nurse and that Olwen was in the habit of visiting her every Saturday to wash her hair. They gave their word of honour that they would do Olwen no harm. The shepherd's wife at last agreed to arrange their meeting with her.

Olwen's dress was flame red
red gold and garnets about her neck
yellow her hair as yellow broom
sea foam no whiter than her white skin
her fingers white as water flowers
her eyes bird bright, her swan white breasts
her cheek's blush like foxglove flowers
filled any man with love of her

Four white clovers sprang in her footsteps where she walked. It was for this she was called by the name Olwen. It means White Track.

As soon as Culhwch saw her, he said to her, 'Maiden it is you and you alone I love. Bind your life with mine, my darling, and come away with me.'

'Speak no more such words,' whispered Olwen. 'I cannot go away with you. It is the nature of my father's fate that he will die if I ever marry. But if you go to my father and ask for my hand in marriage, I will give you this advice. Promise to procure for him whatever he will ask of you. Any hesitation will be certain death to you all. It is also certain that my father will now know you are here. You must go to him.'

They went with her to the fortress of Ysbaddaden and entered after her the hugest gate they had ever seen and followed her into the hall of the king of all giants and found him asleep and snoring.

'Greetings, Ysbaddaden King of all Giants.'

'Who speaks?' grunted Ysbaddaden. 'Where are my useless gate-keepers?'

'We are messengers from Arthur seeking the hand of your daughter Olwen for Culhwch son of Cilydd.'

'Why do I bother paying servants, why do I bother feeding attendants? Prop up the forks under my eyelids so I can see my future son-in-law.'

So they propped great pitchforks up under the giant's eyelids. The giant scowled at them with his stone-grey eyes.

'Come back tomorrow,' he thundered.

They turned to leave, but as they did, Ysbaddaden picked up the nearest of the three poisoned spears he had propped beside him and he hurled it at them. Bedwyr caught it and hurled it back. It pierced Ysbaddaden through the kneecap, and Ysbaddaden said:

'Uncivil pest of a son-in-law this
ever the worse I shall walk up hill
the poison spear stings like a wasp sting

damn the smith that forged it
and damn his anvil.'

The following day they came to him again.
'Ysbaddaden King of All Giants, we seek your daughter's
hand for Culhwch.'

'Her four great-grandmothers and her four great-
grandfathers are yet alive. I must ask their counsel. Come
back tomorrow.'

They turned to leave, but as they did, Ysbaddaden
snatched up the second of his poisoned spears and he hurled
it at them. Menw caught it and hurled it back. It pierced
Ysbaddaden in the hollow below his ribs.

'A double damned ungentlemanly son-in-law this
like the bite of a horse leech
the cold iron cuts me
damn the forge that heated it
every time I walk up hill
I'll have heartburn, gut ache
and a wee bit of indigestion even.'

The third day they came to him again. 'Throw no
more spears at us, Ysbaddaden. Seek not your own death
before your time.'

'Where are my servants? Prop up my eyelids with the
forks again.' They did that, and as they did Ysbaddaden
snatched up the third poisoned spear and hurled it at them.
Culhwch caught it and hurled it back. It pierced
Ysbaddaden in the eye ball.

'A bloody cur of a son-in-law if you ask me
the poison iron bites me like a mad dog
against the wind my eyes will water
as long as I live my sight will be a mite less than perfect
severe headaches will plague me
and giddiness at new moon.'

The next day they came to him again. Ysbaddaden said to them, 'Come forward to me, the one who seeks my daughter.' Culhwch came forward. 'I will set you tasks, and when you have accomplished them you will be married to my daughter. Out of the wood that surrounds my fortress, a field must be cleared and the brush burnt and plowed under. That field must be sowed with grain. It must sprout, ripen, be harvested, and be ground into corn, and all this must be accomplished by the dew fall of tomorrow's first light. This will be the making of your wedding feast.'

'This will be easy for me, though you might think it difficult,' said Culhwch.

Ysbaddaden next expounded an extraordinary rigmarole of completely impossible requirements, which included no fewer than nine of The Thirteen Treasures of Britain[14] and The Birds of Rhiannon. One requirement could not be fulfilled without the completion of the next, and each required the help of some ancient hero whose help seemed impossible to obtain. In this way Ysbaddaden thought to preserve his life, which would be forfeit if Olwen were ever to marry.

But whatever Ysbaddaden asked, Culhwch agreed to perform, saying 'this will be easy for me, though you might think it difficult.' Finally Ysbaddaden set the hardest task of all. It was that his hair and beard must be trimmed. No more than Culhwch had asked Arthur, you would think. But no scissors, razor or comb in the world would serve except those that hung between the ears of the giant boar Twrch Trwyth. No one could hunt him but Mabon,[15] son of Modron, the greatest of all huntsmen, stolen when he was three days old from between his mother and the wall, prisoned and lost beyond the reach of love or war.

But Culhwch said, 'That will be easy for me, though you might think that is difficult. And with the help of my kinsman Arthur, I will perform all these tasks.'

They returned to Arthur and with all his company

Twrch Trwyth (toorich trooith)

they set out to seek Mabon. They went first to the oldest
bird of the forest, the Blackbird of Cilgwri, and Gwrhyr the
Interpreter of Tongues addressed him:

'Wise and ancient Bird of the Forest
Bird of the Forest, know you aught of Mabon
Mabon who, when he was three days old was stolen
stolen from between his mother and the wall?'

And the bird replied:
'In my first feather I first came here
to these green woods where I make my home
to keep the sharp edge on my beak
I found an old smith's anvil for a sharpening stone
now only this scrap of the anvil remains
though no hammer beat it but my beak alone
but in all these years past and gone
I never heard of this man Mabon.
But if anyone would know, it would be the Stag of
    Rhedynfre.'

So they set out to find him, and Gwrhyr addressed him,
saying:
'Wise and ancient Stag of the Mountain
Stag of the Mountain, know you aught of Mabon
Mabon who, when he was three days old was stolen
stolen from between his mother and the wall?'

And the Stag replied:
'A greenhorn buck I first came here
when this ancient oak was a verdant sprout
I have seen it stretch forth a hundred boughs
I have seen it wither, I have seen it rot
till only this stump of the oak remains
and that no bigger than my forefoot
but in all these years, past and gone
I never heard of this man Mabon.
But if anyone would know, it would be the Eagle of
    Gwernabwy.'

27

They went to the eagle, and Gwrhyr addressed him:
> 'Wise and ancient Eagle of Kingdoms
> Eagle of Kingdoms, know you aught of Mabon
> Mabon who, when he was three days old was stolen
> stolen from between his mother and the wall?'

And the eagle replied:
> 'Long and since when I first came here
> this crag of mine was a crag indeed
> every evening I could peck at the stars
> as they whirled in their fires about my head
> my talons have worn the rock away
> to this rump of a boulder on which I perch
> but in all those years past and gone
> I never heard of this man Mabon.
> But if anyone would know, it would be the Salmon
> of Llyn Llyw.'

So they went to the salmon, and Gwyrhyr addressed him:
> 'Wise and ancient Salmon of Wisdom
> Salmon of Wisdom, know you aught of Mabon
> Mabon who when he was three days old was stolen
> stolen from between his mother and the wall?'

And the salmon replied:
> 'I will tell you as much as I know
> and that is more than any other can tell
> I have swum east, I have swum west
> I have swum in the deeps below Gloucester's walls
> and there heard sighing and lamentation
> as never was heard since the world began
> that you may believe that this was Mabon
> I will ferry you straight to the dark prison

Cei and Gwrhyr rode astride the salmon's shoulders until they reached the walls of the dark prison at Caer Loyw, which is now called Gloucester. They called to the prisoner within: 'Who are you here confined that cries and laments so sadly?' And learning that this indeed was

Mabon, they rescued him by force of Arthur's soldiers and continued on their quest with him. They accomplished every difficult feat that had been set them by Ysbaddaden in procuring the dogs, the leashes and all else necessary to hunt the giant boar Twrch Trwyth.

They sent Menw of the Many Skills into Ireland to ascertain the whereabouts of Twrch Trwyth. It was not hard to get news of him, he had already laid waste one third of Ireland. Menw, learning that Twrch Trwyth had made a lair for himself upon the Accursed Ridge, turned himself into a great hawk. He hoped to make off with the razor, comb or scissors that hung between the ears of Twrch Trwyth, the only implements that could be used to trim the hair and beard of Ysbaddaden.

As he sped towards the Accursed Ridge he could see against the skyline the hump of Twrch Trwyth's back from many miles' distance. Some say Twrch Trwyth had been a king turned by God into a boar for his sins, some say he was a kind of god or demon himself, but he was bigger than seven horses, more ferocious than seven lions, his lust for destruction grew seven times the greater with every seven men he destroyed. Seven of his young dwelt with him.

As Menw fluttered swiftly the length of the enormous, black bristled spine, there gleamed before him the great comb, the razor and scissors, silver bright and long as spears. Between the two huge ears that quivered to the east and west of him like two black sails, he was able to grasp no more than one hair. Even so poison from the boar spattered upon him. He was marked by it till the day of his death.

Arthur assembled the warriors of the three islands of Britain and of their adjacent islands and of France, Brittany, Normandy and the Land of Summer. It was with these multitudes that Arthur came to the Accursed Ridge. Whatever approach the Irish armies made in a day and a night, another fifth of Ireland was destroyed by Twrch

Trwyth. In a new day, Arthur's armies marched toward Twrch Trwyth in their turn, and every step of their advance was death and misery to them.

Arthur sent Gwrhyr the Interpreter to parley with Twrch Trwyth, and Twrch Trwyth gave him this reply: 'By the name of the God who caused me this grief, I have nothing to say to Arthur. He will never get the razor, comb or scissors while I am alive. Tomorrow I will swim to Britain, and there I will wreak such destruction as will give you cause to rue that ever you hunted me out.'

And so it was. The next day Twrch Trwyth swam ashore with his young in West Wales. Throughout the length and breadth of Britain, Mabon the son of Modron, the greatest huntsman in the world, hunted him with the two enchanted dogs that had been obtained for him by the questing of Arthur's knights. And in that hunting, Twrch Trwyth slew many of Arthur's greatest heroes. Finally, Mabon hunted Twrch Trwyth to the shores of the Severn, and there Arthur and the champions of Britain fell upon him, and together they managed to drive him into deep waters. Mabon snatched the razor from between his ears. Cyledyr the Wild carried off the scissors. But before anyone could grasp the comb Twrch Trwyth was able to regain his footing, and reaching land neither horse nor hound could keep up with him until he reached Cornwall.

Whatever hardship Arthur and his warriors had had from Twrch Trwyth before was but play to the taking of the comb. But take it they did at last. They drove Twrch Trwyth into the sea. And where he went from that time is not known.

Arthur then obtained and performed all that Ysbaddaden had set them. Even the blood of the Tar Black Witch daughter of the Ice White Witch from the Valley of Grief in the north of Hell Arthur obtained in the fulfilment of his promise to Culhwch.

So it was that they returned to the court of Ysbaddaden. They clipped and shaved Ysbaddaden. They shaved his flesh and skin to the bone, and the two ears from his head. 'Have you been shaved, Ysbaddaden?' asked Culhwch. 'Is your daughter Olwen now mine?'

'I have been shaved,'' said Ysbaddaden, 'Olwen is now yours. Though but for Arthur, you never would have gained her. Now is the time to end my life.'

They cut the head from Ysbaddaden then. That night Culhwch slept with Olwen. As long as he lived, she was his only wife.

WINTER

sharp wind
stark hill
scant shelter
unforded ford
frozen lake
a single stem
would bear a man
wave on wave
drowns the shore
high cries
from the steep slope
hard even to stand
for a man outside
cold lakebed
before the winter
reeds withered
stalks broken
harsh wind
branches bare
cold bed of fishes
under ice cover
starved stag
bearded reeds
short evening

trees bent
falling snow
white cloak
warriors make
no foray
cold lake
of warmthless colour
falling snow
hoar frost
idle shield
on a spent man's shoulder
shrill wind
grass freezing
falling snow
on the skin of the ice
billowing wind
through close trees
a shield sits well
on a well man's shoulder
falling snow
the valley fills
warriors go to war
but I shall not go
a wound forbids it

Welsh, author unknown;
c. eleventh century

THE MADNESS OF SUIBHNE

St Ronan was one of the great saints of the early Celtic church, almost as famous in his day as St Patrick and St Columba. He must have got about a bit, for they say, in the wee town of Innerleithen in the Scottish Borders where I lived for years, years ago, that St Ronan drove out a one-legged devil there who was pestering the people. But ancient Irish books record this following story about St Ronan and how he cursed the young king Suibhne.[1]

Ronan was measuring out the site for a church he planned on the shores of a loch in Erin at the place called Cill Luinnidh, and this was in the lands of Suibhne, son of Colman, king of Dál n Araidhe.

Suibhne, seated at his own table, was drinking when he heard the sound of Ronan's bell. And learning what this trespassing cleric was about, he arose in red rage and rushed headlong to drive St Ronan from his lands. Suibhne's wife Eorann grasped the fringes of his crimson cloak to halt him as he shoved past her. But Suibhne's royal brooch of white silver set with gold tugged free from the cloth, the cloak was left in Eorann's hands and Suibhne ran, stark naked, out of his house in his frenzy to be rid of Ronan.

Now Suibhne burst out of the bushes as Ronan was singing a prayer to the King of Earth and Heaven, and snatching from Ronan his beautiful book of psalms, Suibhne hurled it into the cold brown all-concealing waters of the loch. The book sank. Suibhne was laying hands on Ronan then, in the rage that roared in him like fire. And you'd think that Ronan's last hour was at hand, for he was a skinny old man held together with cold water and prayer and Suibhne was a great hairy ruffian of a king, who'd always had all the mead and meat that he could swallow and who was used to kill for the least offence. But as he was going at the saint like a terrier at a rat, there was heard the shout of a messenger bearing news of a great

Suibhne (súvni)   Cill Luinnidh (kill linny)
Dal n Araidhe (del narry)

battle to be fought at Magh Rath. Suibhne went off with this messenger without further ado, leaving Ronan rubbing his bruises in sadness for the loss of his holy book, and in sorrow for the evil of the world.

After a day and night, an otter came clambering out of the loch bringing the beautiful psalter back to Ronan, not a line nor a letter marred, not a colour blurred.

But Suibhne continued in his usual ways, skirmishing, truce breaking and dealing plain murder, till the day he met again with Ronan as Ronan was walking with eight singers singing psalms and shaking holy water on the people. Some of the water splashed on Suibhne, and he, thinking they were making jest of him, cast a spear at one of Ronan's singers and killed him as he stood. And Suibhne cast a spear at Ronan also and the spear struck the bell that Ronan always wore around his neck. The spear was turned by this bell and flew high into the air.

Ronan put his curse on Suibhne then, saying, 'I pray to God that as high as that spear flew you yourself may soar among the weathers upon the wings of your own distress. I pray that you may find no trust. And I pray you get your death at last by the death you gave my singer.'[2]

It was not long after that Suibhne's mind was filled with night and chaos, with river-rushing, wind-roaring, wave-crashing easelessness. He hated all the places he had loved. He yearned for all the places he had never known. His hands flapped. His legs fluttered. His heart trembled. His eyes showed him no truth. And he fled under the curse of Ronan, believing himself a bird or a sprite of air.

His feet seldom touched the ground, so flighty was his flight, dew drops he left unshattered in his light, high stepping. He did not cease his furious leaping till there was not a shore, glen, hillock, crag, moor, quagmire, spinney, little wood, forest or patch of briars in Erin that he did not cross in his first day's madness.

Thereafter[3] his days and nights were spent among barren rocks and among the branches of trees, until he came

Magh Rath (my ra)

to Glen Bolcán. This was the glen where every madman used to go after they had endured a year of madness. This was the place of which all mad people were most fond. For in this glen there were four passes to the clear wind, a green wood of bushy trees, pure springs and streams gurgling along sandy beds. Every kind of wild fruit was there, with garlic, acorns and cresses. After a year in the wilds, the body of Suibhne was torn with branches and pierced with brambles. His skin was tighter on his ribs than the skin of a goat-skin drum. What parts of him were not blue with cold were red streaked with his blood. And there, perched in the branches of a yew tree, he made this lamentation.

> 'Heart of my thought, cruel this life
> after the fine fat days I knew as king
> a bare year in the arms of the trees
> who once enjoyed the arms of beautiful women'

After seven years the nobles of Erin managed to trace the whereabouts of Suibhne. So they sent his brother-in-law Loingseachán to him, his greatest friend. And Loingseachán sought him through the most distant glens, till he found him at last perching among branches. But for all Loingseachán's wheedling and kind words, Suibhne would not come down, for a great fear possessed him in his madness. Loingseachán said to him:

> 'Sorrowful fate, Suibhne
> this that has befallen you
> pleasureless life
> you bird of hunger
> who once wore silk
> who once went prancing
> on mettled gold-bridled steeds
> beautiful generous women beside you
> young men and sages in your company
> fine hounds, not a few
> servants to serve you at your lifted finger

many a gold cup you quaffed of wine
many a horn of frothy drink
now look at you, you rag-tag
you crow
from wilderness to wilderness
hopping and scrambling'

And Suibhne replied: 'Enough from you, Loingseachán, such is my sorrowful fate indeed. What news can you give me?'

'Your father is dead,' said Loingseachán.

'A fountain of remorse is that,' said Suibhne.

'Your mother is dead,' said Loingseachán.

'A gale of ill that too,' said Suibhne.

'Your brother has been killed,' said Loingseachán.

'A wound in my side is that,' said Suibhne.

'Your daughter is no longer alive,' said Loingseachán.

'A small knife in my heart is that,' said Suibhne.

'Your little son is dead that used to smile into your fatherly face,' said Loingseachán.

'That,' said Suibhne, 'is the blow that brings a man to the ground.'

He fell, in his grief, from his perch among the branches then. Loingseachán put his arms around him and bound Suibhne with fetters, so he could leap no more. It was only then Loingseachán told him his family were not dead, and he took him to Dál nAraidhe, where after a month and a fortnight among his own people Suibhne returned to his senses.

All would have been well, but for an old woman about the house who, in spite of strict orders not to talk to Suibhne, did so. It was at a time when everyone else was in the harvest fields that the old woman reminded Suibhne of his troubles and of his sin by asking him of how it was when he was mad, and she caused his madness to return to him. She said to him, 'Could you not leap me a leap such as the leaps you leapt when you were mad?'

Loingseachán (lýn khe khaun)

And casting his clothes aside, away he went, as stark and mad as ever he was, leaping and leaping till he crossed the sea by Ailsa Craig and came to Scotland. It was there he met with another madman called Fear Caille, Man of the Wood. They agreed to be friends. Fear Caille said to him:

'Who first shall hear heron's voice
across dark waters
or clear call of cormorant
or rise of woodcock
or plover's warning note
or twig snap in silence
or bird shadow below the sun
shall warn the other.'

One thing became clear to these two madmen in their friendship, they became sure of how they each would die, and to meet their deaths they bade farewell to each other and went their own ways.

Returning to Erin, Suibhne met Mo Ling the scholar, who put him under a promise that no matter how far he wandered in a day, he would return each evening to him, that he might write down the story of Suibhne.

Mo Ling's milkmaid was told to give Suibhne food, and her habit was to thrust her heel into a pat of cow-dung and fill it with warm milk for Suibhne. And at evening, Suibhne would come fearfully and furtively to drink. Stretched out upon the ground, he would lap at the milk.

But the milkmaid's husband became jealous of Suibhne. Gossip spread, nurtured by the women about the place, till one day his sister shouted at him, 'You pitiful cuckold! Don't you care that your wife is in the hedge with a naked madman?' The man ran out of the house with a spear and cast it at Suibhne. It entered his body above the left nipple as he lay lapping at the milk among the cow-dung, and it left his body by way of his backbone, which it broke in two.

Fear Caille (far killy)

Mo Ling was told, and he brought the priest to Suibhne, where he lay dying. They gave him last rites. His own full awareness returned to him.

'Had I known who you were,' said the milkmaid's husband, 'I would never have wounded you, however great the harm you had done me.'

'I swear to you, man,' said Suibhne, 'I never harmed you in any way, or any on the ridge of the world, since Ronan's curse sent me from my senses.'

'Christ's curse upon you that killed poor Suibhne!' said Mo Ling. 'A short life here and hell beyond it.'

'That's no use to me,' said Suibhne, 'the door of my death is before me, thanks to his spear cast.' Suibhne died. They built him a cairn in that place, and Mo Ling the scholar, prophesied Suibhne's entry into paradise.

'Beloved is the man under this cairn,' said Mo Ling. 'How often we talked in the quiet of evening. That pool of water where he often drank and where he would eat the watercresses shall now be called Suibhne's Well. Beloved will be every wilderness through which Suibhne travelled.'

Based on *Buile Suibhne*;
Original manuscript, twelfth-century Irish

THE SPOILS OF ANNWN

THE MYSTERIOUS POEM, 'PREIDDEU ANNWN', RECOUNTS A raid on the otherworld the British Celts call 'Annwn'[1] *or* '*Annwfn*'. This raid was carried out by King Arthur to obtain the Cauldron of Inspiration and Rebirth. This Cauldron was concealed and guarded amongst the various fortresses mentioned. These fortresses may represent stations of the soul in its journey after death, between lives, or while alive, in a bardic vision. The speaker in the poem is Taliesin, who has been everywhere, at all times and in all things; for at root Taliesin, like Arthur and the other characters here, is a deity, and an inspired bard would speak as Taliesin.

praise to the Power who orders Highest Heaven
who to the shores of Earth extends dominion
fast in the Turning Castle Gwair was prisoned
in Caer Sidi by Pwyll and Pryderi's malison
no one before Gwair[2] suffered the like confinement
the chain that bound him was the boundless ocean
among the wealth of the dead his lamentation
and dolorous his song till the day of doom
we went there three times the fill of the ship Prydwen
none returned from Spiral Castle but seven men
of all that company
none but seven returned from Caer Sidi[3]

am I not worthy of fame and honour in song?
in the Four-Cornered Castle four times spun
who else can say what primal word was spoken?
from the Cauldron warmed by the breath of the Nine
    Virgins
from the pearl-rimmed Cauldron of the Lord of Annwn
that will boil no coward's repast nor one forsworn
to these will be brought a death sharp and shining
by the sword that will be left in Lleminawg's[4] right hand
in the Gate of Coldness horns of light were burning

Annwn (anoon)   Caer Sidi (kye er sithee)
Lleminawg (hlem ín og)

in that high campaign of the King we were his companions
none returned from the Castle of Revels but seven men
all others died
none but seven returned from Caer Vendiwid[5]

am I not worthy of fame and song forever?
in the Four-Cornered Castle and the Island of the Strong
    Door
where shadows and the darkness meet together
and bright wine brims over in every beaker
three times the fill of Arthur's ship we crossed the waters
none but seven returned from the Castle of the Rulers
none but seven returned from Caer Rigor

I allow the kings of story little honour
who beyond the Glass Castle[6] saw not the prowess of
    Arthur
six thousand men arrayed along those ramparts
with their watchmen we could scarce confer
three times the fill of Prydwen we sent with Arthur
none but seven returned from the Castle of Treasure
none but seven returned from Caer Golur[7]

little praise to men of little valour
who know neither the day nor its Author
of Cwy's[8] birth they know not the hour
or who from the Dales of Defwy was his barrier
they know not the Brindled Ox[9] nor its halter
nor the seven score hand-breadths of its collar
ah when we went with Arthur, mournful the memory
none but seven returned from Caer Vandwy[10]

men of no courage merit no praise
they know not on what day the Ruler arose
nor in what hour born the Owner was
nor of what kind was his Silver-Headed Beast
ah when we went with Arthur, grief of armed men
none but seven returned from Caer Ochren[11]

Based on the poem by Thomas ap Einion;
Welsh, thirteenth century

Cwy (coy)   Vandwy (van doy)
Caer Vendiwid (kyre vendée wid)

II

WIZARDS AND HISTORY

Ancient Celtic history was not concerned so much with facts as with royal or noble ancestry, explanation of place names and prophecies fulfilled. Geoffrey of Monmouth, Walter Map, the Venerable Bede, Nennius and other early chronicler did not hesitate to include fable and mythology whenever facts were sparse. But fabulous as they are, they have a charm of their own and a truth of their own, and record some of the oral tradition of their time that would otherwise now be lost to us.

Genuine traditional histories such as the *Gododdin*, preserved in oral heritage since the fifth century AD and finally written down in the thirteenth, display a more personally involved aesthetic which in the later stories here, becomes romantic.

THE THREE PLAGUES OF BRITAIN

LONG AND AGO AND BEFORE THE DAYS OF ARTHUR THE kingdom of Britain was ruled by Lludd,[1] son of Beli Mawr. He ruled wisely and well, and extended the walls of the capital city—called after him, Caer Ludd, and later Caer Lundein and later yet, London.

Lludd arranged that his favourite brother Llefelys should marry the daughter of the king of France. And so Llefelys did, and in due course inheriting the French crown, he ruled that land well and wisely.

But there came upon Britain three plagues the like of which had never been known in the land before. And the first of these plagues was the coming of the Corannieid.[2] The Corannieid were a race of wizards whose chief power was knowing at once whatever words were spoken anywhere in the land. Even the softest whisper, if borne upon the air, the Corannieid knew of it. For that reason, none could harm them.

And the second plague was a great shout[3] or cry that every May-day Eve wailed out above every hearth in Britain. All men it utterly unmanned, all women with child it made miscarry, all children it felled, all animals, forests, earth and waters it left defiled and wasted.

And the third plague was of this nature. No matter how great a supply of victuals and drink the king's court might prepare, even if it were enough for a whole year, the only part ever consumed was that part consumed in one night, the first night of the feast. Anything left would vanish, leaving neither drop nor crumb nor any trace at all.

In despair, Lludd took ship for France to consult his brother. He told none where he was going, and to his brother he spoke only through a long, copper horn, lest any of his words, sounding in the air, might reach the Corannieid.

But only adverse, pugnacious and contrary words would pass through that horn, no matter what the brothers

Lludd (hleethe)   Llefelys (hle véllis)   Corannieid (ko rán yied)

actually were saying. Llefelys knew then that a demon was obstructing the horn between them. He ordered the horn cleansed with wine. And so it was. The wine washed the demon out.

Now that they could understand each other aright, Llefelys advised his brother as to the use of certain poisoned mites, which, if dropped in the waters of Britain would poison only the Corannieid and leave all others hale and hearty.

'The cause of the second plague,' said Llefelys, 'is dragon-conflict. That is the scream of a dragon that you hear.' And Llefelys directed Lludd how to deal with this.

'And the cause of the third plague,' said Llefelys, 'is a wizard who is a thief. A food thief. A very hungry magician, I should say.'

Llefelys directed his brother how to proceed in this predicament also.

So when Lludd returned home he sprinkled the poison mites into the wells and waters of Britain. The Corannieid took sick from them. It was not long till they all were dead.

Then, following the detailed instructions of Llefelys, Lludd had measurements taken to determine the exact centre of the island of Britain. Oxford is where it was found to be. There he had a great pit dug and filled with the finest mead that could be procured, and with a huge sheet of silk, he covered it over.

Two dragons appeared then, in aerial combat. And with great splutterings of fire and venom they attacked each other across the skies, clawing and rending each the other until, in exhaustion, their wings were failing and they could fight no more. They fell upon the silk sheet, and down they went into the pool of mead.

But the creatures that fell into the pool of mead were no longer dragons ... but little pigs! They drank and guzzled at the mead until they fell fast asleep. Lludd had them wrapped in the silk and carried away to Mount Snowdon, where, in two stone coffers they were buried deep.

Now to deal with the wizard thief, Lludd made ready to keep watch in his own palace while a great feast was prepared and laid at table. And as Llefelys had warned him of the wizard's sleep-charm, he also had a great tub of icy water at hand.

About three in the morning, a beautiful air of music[4] came wafting through the halls, with an inexpressible drowsiness about it. But Lludd, as his eyelids drooped, dashed himself into the icy water and was able thus to combat the sleep until the charm ceased.

He could see then an armoured man, cramming all the dainties and fine drink into the basket he had with him. A bottomless basket it must have been, for food enough for a year and a day went into it. Lludd laid into the scoundrel with his sword, and the thief and he fought together till their two swords were blunted against their two shields and their two shields were notched like new cheeses on a Friday. They fell next to the grips of wrestling and wrestled. They put wounds on each other you could whistle through, and bruises like plums. But in the end, Lludd got a fierce and royal hold on the intruder that soon made the rascal call for quarter.

'Why should I give you any mercy after all the wrong you have done me?' said Lludd.

The wizard swore not only to make full recompense but also to serve King Lludd from that day forward.

And this is the tale called The Three Plagues of Britain. And so it ends.

VORTIGERN'S TOWER

LONG AND AGO AND BEFORE THE DAYS OF ARTHUR, Vortigern,[1] Earl of Gwent, made himself King of the Britons by treachery and murder. And in his greed for power, he made the greatest error in Celtic history. He enlisted the aid of the Saxons and gave them land in the north of England, their first foothold.

Ah, but the Saxons stopped not there. They captured London, York, Lincoln and Winchester, slaying as wolves slay sheep unshepherded, and Vortigern fled before them into Wales.

There he took counsel with his chief wizards. And they gave him prime advice: to build a stronghold. Upon Mount Snowdon was the favoured site, the highest peak in the land. But whatever the king's masons built by day was swallowed into the earth by night. His wizards counselled him further, saying nothing would hold the stones firm but the blood of a boy who had never had a father.

So search was made, and such a boy was found, in the town now called Carmarthen, where a lady of noble birth, and a nun, moreover, had conceived a child to a spirit of the air. For as the learned Apuleius[2] reports: 'Certain spirits between the earth and moon partake of the nature of both men and angels.' Surely such a spirit had fathered the boy they brought to Vortigern. Merlin was his name.[3]

No word or gesture betrayed the boy as sentence of death was read to him, and his blood required of him to hold firm the stones.

But he said: 'Bid your wizards come forward and I will reveal their ignorance to you, oh King.'

They were brought at once, for the boy spoke with power. He enquired of the wizards: 'Since you claim knowledge, what lies below these foundations?'

The wizards were abashed and answered not a word.

'Bid your workmen dig deeper, oh King, and they will pierce to the waters of a great pool.'

They did. And so it was. Waters filled all the land about.

'Drain these,' said Merlin. 'You will find two huge stones, and in them, asleep, one red dragon and one white.'

They did. And so it was. And the dragons awoke, flapped ponderously into the skies, and there attacked each other, fire and claw, the white dragon and the red.

Then Merlin drew in the breath of prophecy, and spoke these words as the bards relate:

'alas, alas the red dragon[4]
for the hour of his doom is rung
for the red is our own portent
as the white is the Saxons'
and they will be our oppression
sore and long
our valleys they will pillage and our mountains
the courses of our streams will course with blood
the churches of our faith will be razed and ruined
and stilled will be the worship of our God
until the wild boar bear the crown from Cornwall
to rule the ocean's islands and the forests of Gaul
till even the house of Romulus will tremble
his last fate no seer will foretell
his name will be the fame of all his people
his deeds as meat to those that recite his praise
six of his descendants will bear his mantle
but after these the German worm will rise'

Now this is the first prophecy of Merlin, and it foretells the coming of Arthur. And all came to pass here foretold. As for Vortigern, some say he died by fire in the coming of Aurelius,[5] the brother of Uthur Penndragon, who sired or fostered Arthur. But some say Vortigern escaped to Brittany, and there became a saint, St Gwrtheyrn. And so this story ends.

ARTHUR, THE EARLY LEGEND

IT IS NOW GENERALLY ACKNOWLEDGED THAT THE LEGEND OF
Arthur is based historically on the deeds of a war leader of
the Britons against invading Anglo-Saxons about the sixth
century. But the legend as we've become familiar with it
does not appear in the earliest sources. It grows rapidly
after the Norman conquest, and Arthur emerges with
qualities culled from earlier mythology in readiness to
become the fount of chivalry and the inspiration of the
Grail Quest to foster courtly manners and *amour courtois*.
The knights of his court and the kings and giants of the
tales are liberally filched from Celtic legend and are, in
origin, often Celtic deities. Arthur himself takes for the
medieval heart the role played by Gwydion in the more
ancient British tales, or by Fionn mac Cumhaill in Ireland
and Gaelic Scotland.

The legend of Arthur has never died. In fact, the legend
has been so tampered with, by the meistersingers of the old
Germans, the troubadours of Provence, the romancers of
the High Middle Ages, the romantic poets, painters and
composers of the nineteenth century, and by the novelists
and film-makers of our own, that the outline of the early
legend may well be worth retelling, in its simplicity.

Now this is not the Arthur of ancient Celtic myth,
who frees captives from the otherworld, and is, in turn,
freed himself from the Dark Prison under Stone. Nor is it
the High King dreamed by later poets in a Camelot of
eternal jousting. But it is the Arthur of the twelfth-century
vision, at the beginning of the English legend.

After Vortigern had betrayed Britain to the Teutonic
invaders, Ambrosius Aurelius rallied the Britons, became
king and after long, hard conflict defeated Hengist, ruler of
the Saxons. Ambrosius Aurelius then set about the repair of
the churches and towns of Britain which had been
destroyed, and wishing to make a monument to those of

his companions who had died in the wars, he consulted the finest craftsmen in stone and wood. They advised him to enquire of Merlin, the same who had been prophet to Vortigern. Messengers were sent in search of him, and they found him in Gwent, near the fountain of Galabes.

So he was brought to Aurelius who, wishing to hear some marvels, asked Merlin to prophesy. Merlin refused, saying:

'Mysteries should never be revealed save in time of great need. If I were to tell of them for lightness or laughter, the spirit that informs me would forsake me. But if you would make a monument of eternal value, send for the Dance of the Giants that is on Mount Killare in Ireland.'

Aurelius burst out laughing, for how could anyone move the Giant's Dance, a massive stone circle and from so far away. What was wrong with British stones at all?

But Merlin said: 'There is a particular virtue in those stones, for giants in ancient times transported them to Ireland from Africa. And water poured over them becomes imbued with healing power to cure every ill, by means of bathing therein, or by herbal concoctions thereof.'

So it was agreed. And Uthur, brother of Aurelius set out with troops and with Merlin to Ireland. And by force of arms and by Merlin's art they transported the stones to Salisbury Plain, where they stand, as Stonehenge, to this day.

In the fullness of his reign, it came to pass that Aurelius was poisoned by one Eoppa[1], who had posed as a doctor to him. And at his death appeared a star of brightness, from which a ray burst forth into a ball of fire like a dragon with two rays from its mouth, one reaching to Gaul and the other towards Ireland, ending in seven smaller rays. Merlin, knowing by this of the King's death and of many other things to come, gave Uthur such advices as enabled him to take the throne. Aurelius was buried at Stonehenge, and Uthur was crowned king. His name from that time was Uthur Penndragon, or Dragon-Master, because of the portent displayed by the sky.

Uthur Penndragon was overtaken by a passionate desire for Igerna wife of Gorlois King of Cornwall. He made war on him. Merlin, because of his foreknowledge, undertook to create upon Uthur the semblance of Gorlois, and by his skills he so worked this magic that none could tell Uthur from Gorlois. And so Uthur was able to gain entry to the castle of Tintagel, and to Igerna's chamber, while Gorlois was away with his troops. In that lovemaking Arthur was conceived.

About this time Gorlois was killed in battle. And messengers sent to inform Igerna of his death were dismayed and most astounded to see the likeness of their dead master seated at her side. Uthur, skilfully dissembling, embraced the fair Igerna and left as if to take up arms again. But as soon as they were out of sight, Merlin returned Uthur to his own shape. Siege was laid to Tintagel and the castle fell to Uthur, and likewise Igerna, who in time became his wife. And Arthur, unlawfully begotten, became lawful heir to the throne.

So Uthur reigned, until his death. Arthur his son succeeded him. And this young man proved such a fine leader that he was able to accomplish what none of his forebears had ever achieved: a decisive and lasting victory against the Saxons.

Wielding heroically his sword Caliburn that had been forged in the mysterious Isle of Avalon, he put the foe to rout at the Battle of Mount Badon. And, after taking to wife the beautiful Guinevere (the old stories say he married three queens, all named Guinevere), Arthur extended his dominion to Ireland, Iceland, Scotland, Norway and Gaul.

He then set up his main court at Caerleon on Usk, in Gwent near the Severn. There vassal kings would come to pay him homage in his hall of splendour. There were gathered about the young king the finest knights, the learned and the skilled. There ladies and queens bore white doves in their hands, the least of their attendants clad in ermine. There sounded from Yule to Yule the music of instruments and voices.

The custom was that no lady would grant her love to one whose valour was not thrice proved in combat. It is said that this kept the knights upon their mettle and the ladies chaste.

Word of Arthur's prowess reached the Emperor Lucius in Rome, who haughtily demanded tribute. By way of reply Arthur assembled his forces to invade the territory of Rome, defeating the Emperor's army at a great battle in Gaul. He would have marched on Rome itself, but word reached him that his nephew Mordred, in whose charge he had left the rulership of Britain, had in his absence treacherously made alliance with the Saxons against him.

So Arthur returned to Britain without delay. He confronted the combined hosts of the Germanic forces, the Irish, the Picts and Mordred's men at the Battle of Camlan, where as the chronicler Nennius attests: 'In a single onslaught of Arthur's there fell to the ground nine hundred and sixty men, and no one overthrew them but himself alone.' Among the multitudes that were slain on both sides, Mordred died in that dreadful conflict. Arthur himself, severely wounded, gave up the throne to Constantine son of Cador Duke of Cornwall, and was borne away to the Isle of Avalon for the healing of his wounds.

So runs the early legend of the *rex quondam atque futurus*, the once and future king for, never dying, he might at any time return from the Island of the Apple Trees in the hour of his country's need.

THE STORY OF THE GODODDIN

THE FOREGOING VERSION OF THE LEGEND OF ARTHUR SETS much of the activity in southwest England and South Wales. But in fact, Arthur is equally associated with the north of England, and even more so with southern Scotland, where a number of his actual battles seem to have been fought. Nor is there any part of Britain with a greater number of sites and ancient monuments which once bore or still bear Arthur's name. In fact, the earliest known reference to Arthur is a northerly one, from a poem called the Gododdin, and for a much more accurate picture of how the real Arthur's battles might have been, one could do no better than to sample this classic of early Welsh verse.

It was written around 600 AD by Aneirin,[1] bard to Mynyddawg[2] the Openhanded, ruler of the people called the Gododdin. His kingdom was situated in what is now southeast Scotland, and his capital, Dunedin, is now called Edinburgh. He collected together a retinue of the finest young warriors, three hundred of them, and he feasted them lavishly for a year at his expense. The pay of a warrior in those days was plenty of mead, ale, and wine, payable in advance, obviously; and of warriors killed in battle it was said 'they paid for their mead'.

Mynyddawg sent his band of warriors, Aneirin among them, to a disastrous battle at Catterick in Yorkshire. They were to fight the Angles, the men of Deira, for possession of a major strategic point. And off they rode, laughing, to their doom, white horses under them, armoured in the old style of the Romans and bearing spears, javelins, and short swords.

Aneirin says:
men went to Catterick, thirsty for war
the best mead in their honour might have as well been
   poison
three hundred ordered out against an army
after all the celebration, silence

Gododdin (go dóthin)   Aneirin (a ný rin)   Mynyddawg (minná thaug)

and for all the churching of the priests
death their last reward

men went to Catterick at dawn
their own fine fettle was the death of them
yellow the mead poured, sweet and treacherous
year long the minstrelsy, the harp strings never stilled
   let the blood now that rusts their swords
never be scoured

men went to Catterick, they were famous
their wages they drank from gold cups
a twelve month of festivity
three hundred and sixty three warriors with neck bands of
   gold
and of these who so jovially joined battle
three came away
the two war-dogs of Aeron[3]
unyielding Cynon[4]
and myself, soaked in blood, to recount it

Gododdin's highest, on their mountain horses
swan-white stallions, harnessed for heroes
to guard the red gold of Edinburgh
King Mynyddawg sent them
shields shattered
swords slashed
how pale are the faces of the dead

     Aneirin describes the heroes and their various qualities,
one who was known for his generosity to the church and to
minstrels; one who killed a wolf with his bare hands; one
who always rode a bay horse; one whose words held weight
in council; one who was the poet's dearest friend; one
always known for his kindness, who was loved by everyone.

     and Caradawg[5] and Madawg
     Pyll and Ieuan
     Gwgawn and Gwiawn
     Gwynn and Cynfan

Cynon (kuh non)

and Peredur[6] of the steel weapons
Gwawrddur and Aeddan

And in the first verse of the whole poem, Aneirin describes
an unnamed young soldier:

man's mettle
youth's years
fearless famed
lad astride
a sturdy steed
long maned
lightly shielded
bright sworded
gold fringed boy
unmarried
his blood gushed
his corpse unburied
was victuals for crows

Based on *Book of Aneirin*,
preserved in the thirteenth century.
The original poem consists of more than 1200 lines

Peredur (pere deer)

MICHAEL SCOT

OF ALL THE WIZARDS IN THE LONG ENCHANTED HISTORY OF
the Scottish borders, the most highly reputed must certainly
be Michael Scot. But in the pages of plain fact, he is
recorded as a leading intellectual of the thirteenth century
in western Europe, who lectured at the universities of Paris
and Toledo and was noted as the translator of Avicenna,[1]
Averroes and Aristotle. He was one of the forefathers of
experimental method, and a leading authority on alchemy,
astrology, meteorology, and medicine.

He was called to become adviser to the Holy Roman
Emperor himself, Frederick II.[2] It is recounted that the
Emperor Frederick, desiring to test Michael Scot's skill,
demanded of him one day when they were out walking the
distance between the top of a certain tower and the surface of
the sun. Receiving a prompt answer, he noted it and contrived
most secretly to have the tower made somewhat taller. A few
months later he asked Scot the same question and received an
instant answer, correctly adjusted by the exact amount.

Well, such a man made enemies, of course. And for
political or other reasons the poet Dante assigns Michael
Scot (described tersely as 'thin-shanked') to a place in his
'Inferno'.

But whereas historians incline to the view that Michael
Scot died abroad, tradition in his native Scotland asserts
differently. In fact, Border folklore to this day carries a
wealth of anecdotes regarding him. And here is his story, as
I have heard of it.

They say the wizard was born at Balwearie in Fife, in
an old square tower whose ruins are by the road between
Kirkcaldy and Auchtertool. They say he came to his power
one night while working as a mason in Edinburgh.
Returning from some expedition, he and several
companions were overtaken by a fearful storm on a moor
outside the city. As they stumbled through the downpour,

with thunder booming and lightning slicing the sky, they saw across their path come coiling an enormous serpent. A sudden spear of lightning struck it dead before their eyes.

Shortly thereafter they found shelter in a lonely cottage, and related their adventure to the ancient crone who lived there. She requested them, since they would spend the night under her roof, to fetch her the serpent's heart. And as soon as the storm abated this was done. She set the heart to boil in her cauldron. All his friends fell asleep. But Michael feigned sleep and watched while the hag muttered and hummed and sprinkled herbs and oddities into the seething brew.

At length she took the cauldron from the fire and, setting it aside to cool, left the room. Michael arose, tasted the concoction, acquired in that instant universal knowledge and roused his friends to flee. The witch at that very moment was at the work of their destruction. They made their escape.

In the years that followed Michael acquired, from some shadow of time, a great book of power and incantation. Some say it was the book of Solomon himself that he had brought forth out of the darkness. At all events, Michael brought back from Spain and from North America cabalistic wisdom and was the first wizard to wear a robe embroidered with such symbols. Also a strange hat he wore, that he had designed himself made out of blued steel, which he had himself invented also.

And it was Michael Scot that was sent by the people of Scotland to get the date of Shrovetide (that was the Pope's yearly secret) from the Pope in Rome. But Michael left it very late, and had in the end to resort to magic in order to arrive in time. He summoned a steed faster than the wind, faster than a maiden's thought between two lovers, a magic mare indeed. Sea and land were nothing to her.

As they went the horse asked: 'What say the women of Scotland when they smoor³ the fire?'

'Ride in your Master's Name and never mind that,' said Michael.

'A blessing on you and a curse on your teacher,' said the horse. 'What say the women of Scotland when they put their first born to bed?'

'Ride in your Master's Name and let the women of Scotland sleep,' said Michael.

'Forward was the woman who put the first finger in your mouth,' said the horse.

They came to Rome. The Pope, declaring Michael already too late, asked for proof of his identity as Scotland's premier wizard.

Michael retorted: 'The proof is that the shoe on your foot is not your own.'

Well, hidden beneath his long robes the Pope was wearing a woman's shoe. And the Pope, thus convinced of Michael's powers, whispered to him the date of Shrovetide.

Michael Scot's fame spread far and wide, and he set up house at Oakwood Tower not far from Selkirk, not far from Melrose. The country people held him in high regard. He was not a man to irritate. Had he not cleft the Eildon Hills in three with his stick in a moment of exasperation at the steepness of the track he had to climb there? So when he asked a favour, anyone was quick to grant him whatever lay in their means.

But there was one old witch woman who lived near him, who didn't give a fig for his wizardry. He passed her once with his dogs out hunting, and asked for some proof of her power. She snatched his stick from him and slashed him with it thrice. And he became a hare.

'Shoo, Michael, rin or dee,' she cried, laughing, and set his own dogs on him. He was very hard pressed, and had to swim the river and enter his own castle by a drain till he could get back to his own shape. So he planned a revenge for himself, and later sent his servant to Fauldshope where the witch woman dwelt with her family.

He sent with his servant a parchment with these words on it: 'Michael Scot's man cam here for breid and gat nane.' If the servant was given bread, well and good; but if not, he was secretly to lodge the parchment over the lintel of the door.

When the servant came to Fauldshope he got a churlish reply to his request for bread, so he hid the parchment over the door and came away.

That night, when the witch and her family were at supper, oh they had plenty of food, a fiddle came floating through the open window and hovering above the table began to play by itself. It played such a tune that none could forbear to dance. They hopped and skipped and cavorted and leaped and frolicked and stepped and stumbled and staggered till morning. And in the first light the fiddle flew away, leaving them half killed with dancing. So they lost no time in sending round a loaf after that, do you see?

Michael Scot called up a demon once, the biggest demon he had ever managed, who loured over him hundreds of feet high, roaring:

'Give me work or I will rend thee!'

So Michael set him building bridges to the Bass Rock and houses in a single night. But all these usual demon-works he accomplished in the blink of an eye, roaring ever and anon:

'Give me work or I will rend thee!'

Finally Michael set the demon twining ropes of sand to reach the moon, and he's at that to this day. And those little twists you see on the beach, some call them sand worm casts, but we know better.

Now I mentioned that Michael wore a metal hat. He called it a 'cereberium'. He wore it because he knew he would meet his death by reason of a tiny pebble falling on his head. He wore the hat on all occasions, save in church, and it was one day at Mass a wee bit of stone fell from the vault above on to his head. Now it hardly hurt him at all, but when he had it weighed it proved to be of the very weight foretold by the stars. So, returning to his chambers at Oakwood Tower he set his affairs in order and prepared to meet his death.

He prophesied that as his soul left his body a white dove and a black raven would fly to perch on his corpse. Whichever reached his body first would signify the destiny of his soul, the dove for Heaven, the raven for Hell.

Well, it was the dove that won, and Michael Scot is buried in Melrose Abbey, together with his magic book. There's many have tried to dig that up over the years, but none have found it. It is said that a midnight moonbeam at midsummer points to its hiding place. But whether that is so or not, there is, among the abbey ruins, a grave pointed out as the grave of the wizard.

He put a curse once on a family in Brechin sticking his sword into a young oak, saying that when that sword fell their house would fall also. The sword is still there. It was pointed out to me when I was a boy. The oak is a huge old tree now. And there's a tower at Oakwood yet, built in 1602 on the site of the wizard's dwelling by his descendant Robert Scot. It stands in the middle of a farmyard now. I've been to see it, and I've been to Balwearie also, on one of those sweet summer evenings when the bats were aflit about its ivied ruins. Oh, it's got an air about it, and no mistake. There's an old ballad from Stuart days, about some soldiers forced by circumstance to spend the night at Balwearie. It runs:

> what gars ye gaunt, my merry men a'?
> what gars ye look sae eerie?
> what gars ye hing yer heids sae sair?
> by the castle o' Balwearie?[4]

THOMAS THE RHYMER

DRIVING SOUTH FROM EDINBURGH ON THE LAUDER ROAD
you'll come to the small town of Earlston. There's a garage
there called the Rhymer's Filling Station and behind it, half
hidden, the untended ruins of a medieval tower. In that
same tower dwelt during the thirteenth century the poet
and harper Thomas of Earlston, called the Rhymer. His
literary fame rests on his poem 'Sir Tristrem', praised
throughout Europe in its day as the finest version of the
romance of Tristan and Isolde. But the unknown makers of
the Scottish ballads have preserved for us the following
strange legend of Thomas himself.

The ancient thorn they called the Eildon Tree[1] was
always one of Thomas's favourite haunts. He'd take his
harp and while away the summer afternoons by the waters
of Bogle Burn[2] on the slopes of the three-peaked Eildons.[3]
It was always known as an uncanny place, a place where
fortune might wink or scowl. The very place a poet would
choose when at his verses. A feared and honoured place, as
the bards relate:

On a day of days, the Lady came—riding her white horse
between the worlds, she that was Elfland's Queen[4]—to hear
the Rhymer's music for herself.

> her skirt was o' the grass green silk
> her mantle o' the velvet fine
> at ilka tett o' her horse's mane
> hung fifty siller bells and nine

And she that was more beautiful than frost or firelight
gave him good warning. 'Harp and carp,' she said, 'sing
and play, but if you dare to kiss my lips, sure of your body
I will be.'

But he said:
> 'Betide me wel, betide me woe
> that weird sall never daunten me'

And he kissed her rosy lips, all in the shade of the Eildon Tree. In that moment her beauty changed to foulness, her golden hair to straggles of grey, her royal clothes to filthy rags, her face grew skull thin and leaden pale. She beckoned him, and he must needs follow.

> 'Now ye maun gang Thomas,' she said
> 'ye maun rise and gang wi' me
> and ye maun serve me seven years
> through weel or woe as may chance to
>   be'

> she mounted on her milk white steed
> and Thomas he louped on behind
> and aye whenever the bridles rang
> the steed gaed faster than the wynd

And somehow they rode into the hill itself, or into the silence from which all things are born. They crossed the river that runs with the blood that is shed on Earth.

Now when they reached the far bank of that river, the Lady's beauty was restored to her a hundredfold. They rode out into a green and misty landscape where the way branched into three. And she said:

> 'o see ye not yon narrow road
> that's a' beset wi' thorn and briar?
> that is the Path of Righteousness
> and few there be that there aspire

> and see ye not yon wide smooth road
> that's winds across the lily leaven?
> that is the Path of Wickedness
> though many ca' it the Road to Heaven

> and see ye not yon bonny, bonny road
> that winds across the ferny brae?
> that is the path to fair Elfland
> where you and I this night maun gae'

Setting off on that bonniest road, she gave him this advice for his soul's sake, that he would answer none but herself while he was in that land, that was before the world.

Words are weak to tell of Elfland's beauty. But it is said that orchards there are of every fruit, gardens of every flower. Those who have returned speak of buildings more beautiful than churches or castles, yet neither cruel nor holy, but made for the dance that heeds not night or day. Music plays there, of gittern, psaltery, lute and rebec but above all the melting strains and merry notes of the harp, feasting there is without satiety, pleasure without end.

Thomas waited always at the Lady's right hand, passing her this or that as she required. And a handsome manservant to her he made, listening, you may be sure, to the music and songs, the like of which were never made by Adam's kin.

Then the Lady said: 'Now you must leave.'

'How can that be?' said Thomas. 'Scarcely a day since we came here.'

'Ah, but seven full years on Earth have passed,' said she. 'And every seven years we must pay tithe to Hell.[5] If you were to stay I fear the Fiend would choose you. You've served me faithfully. I give you this as your wages. I give you a tongue that will never lie.'[6]

But this pleased Thomas ill:

'My tongue's my ain, my tongue's my ain
a gudely gift you wad gie to me
I durst neither bargain nor speak in hall
nor seek for grace from fair lady'

Yet even as he spoke, Thomas found himself walking towards Earlston in a break of day. Never a lie could he speak from that time forth. His prophecies became famous in all the lands of Scotland, and many are still repeated in the Border Country.[7] 'True Thomas' was the name he gained in many long years.

As a sign at the last his worldly work was done, there came in the gloaming through Earlston to his door-side, a pair of deer. None could drive them away. Neither dogs nor arrows would harm them. A hart and a hind, as white as the white thorn flowers. Then Thomas arose, leaving his guests at table, and followed these white deer into the pure and gathering dark.

From the original romance,
Thomas of Erceldoune, c. fifteenth century

III

THE WISE AND FOOLISH TONGUE

The powers of the bards in aristocratic Celtic society were the powers of praise and satire. Their skill included a command of elaborate metre, and their secret apparently had to do with the acquisition of a voice of power. The bardic heritage of satire has its descendants in the humorous tales of folk heritage, which make light of kings and heroes.

SONG OF THE WIND

ABOUT THE SIXTH CENTURY THERE REIGNED A KING, URIEN, in a kingdom called Rheged, whose capital was the town now known as Carlisle. King Urien's name might well be forgotten today but for his poet, Taliesin, a poet so brilliant that his remaining works are regarded as classics of world literature. This poem *Can y Gwynt*, Song of the Wind, is at once an incantation, a riddle and a song of praise.

unriddle me this, if you can
I was before God's flood
without flesh or vein or bone
headless, footlessly I stride
nothing's child, never born
when my breath stills, I am not dead
no older now, nor ever young
I have no need of beast or man

sea-whitener, forest-piercer
handless I touch a whole field
Time's partner, Youth's partaker
wide as the wide earth is wide
unequalled, masterless, never prisoner
landless, invisible and blind
solitary and brash of manner
gentle, murderous, and without sin
I am no repairer of disorder
I am wet and dry and weak and strong
what am I? that the cold moon fosters
and the ardour of the sun

Urien (eerien)   Taliesin (tal yéssin)

THE BIRTH OF TALIESIN

TALIESIN HAS BECOME A FIGURE OF LEGEND AND HIS WELSH countrymen accord him the title 'Chief of the Bards'. Long long ago the following strange story was first written down concerning his birth. It seems to have more than one level of meaning.

In the days of Arthur, High King of the Britons, there lived a woman of power, named Ceridwen,[1] and her son Afagddu[2] was the ugliest lad in the world. Ceridwen saw there was no way forward for Afagddu unless he could excel in wit or wisdom, but there, as in looks, he was sadly lacking.

So, consulting in her books of knowledge, Ceridwen scoured chapter and verse till among the arcana of Virgil the Gaul, she found the spell for the Cauldron of Inspiration.[3]

She gathered together wheat, honey, incense, myrrh, aloes, precious silver and fluxwort. And these she mixed in the cauldron with the red berries called ruddy gem, that the Welsh call *borfes y Gwion*. And she stirred in the cress known as fabarion and the herb vervain, culled in the rising of the Dog Star. And she set the cauldron to boil as the book directed, to boil one year and one day.

She ordered her servant boy, Gwion Bach, to mind that cauldron, to stir it slow and well and to keep it at the boil. Day in day out he was at that work, till one morning near the year's end three drops splashed on to his finger. All the inspiration intended for Afagddu was in those three drops. Gwion, cooling his scalded finger in his mouth, knew at once the past, the present and the future, knew that Ceridwen meant his death and took to his heels out the door, while the cauldron cracked in a thousand pieces behind him. For all the liquid that remained was deadliest poison.

When Ceridwen heard the crack of the cauldron she at

Ceridwen (Kerídwen)   Afagddu (av ág thee)

once made chase. Gwion became a hare for speed. But she became a hound and followed him the closer. He became a fish to foil the hound. She became an otter and followed him the closer. He became a dove, to foil the otter. She became a hawk, and followed him always the closer. In the failing of his strength at last, he became a wheat groat in a pile of wheat. But she became a black hen, and scuffed at the wheat until she found the one grain that was Gwion Bach, pecked him up and swallowed him whole.

But if all is true that is no lie, that was not the end of him. For in the course of time Ceridwen bore another son, and that son was little Gwion. Such a lovely baby he was, that even she had not the heart to kill him outright, but she bound him into a bag of skins and cast him into the sea.

The sea swept up and the sea swept down and the sea danced after the light moon and the dark, and the bag went wherever the sea went from the time of King Arthur till the time of King Maelgwn, and that was a long time. But the babe aged not one day in that bag or in that time.

At last, near Aberystwyth, the bag was caught in the salmon nets[4] of King Gwyddno.[5] Every May Eve the king was in the habit of granting the salmon rights to one he wished to favour. And this year it was to his own son Elphin he gave the rights. A terrible young wastrel and spendthrift young Elphin was, so they say, who badly needed the salmon for the value of them towards his debts.

He lost no time in wading out where the long nets were staked across the river mouth, where he could see a black something bobbing in the current. He hauled it ashore. Maybe it was jewels, a cask of drink, something of worth. He opened it up.

Out jumped the babe from the mouth of the bag speaking words of power and music, the like of which were never heard in the world before. And because of the light that streamed from the babe's face Elphin gave him the name Taliesin, which means Shining Brow.

Together they returned to Gwyddno's hall. Gwyddno said to Elphin: 'I hope you caught plenty of fish!'

'Better than that, Father,' said Elphin. 'I caught a poet!'

Gwyddno groaned aloud. It was then that Taliesin spoke these words, as the bards relate:

I am Taliesin
I sing perfect metre which will last till the world's end
I know why an echo answers again
why liver is bloody, why breath is black and why silver
   shines
I know why a cow has horns
and why a woman loves a man
why milk is white and holly green
ale bitter and ocean brine
how many spears make a confrontation
how many drops a shower of rain
I know why there are scales on fish and black feet on
   swans

I have been a blue salmon
a dog, a stag, a roebuck on the mountain
a stock, a spade, an axe in the hand
a buck, a bull, a stallion
upon a hill I was grown as grain
reaped and in the oven thrown
out of that roasting I fell to the ground
pecked up and swallowed by the black hen
in her crop nine nights lain
I have been dead, I have been alive, I am Taliesin.'

Gwyddno (gwithno)

THE BATTLE OF THE TREES

OF ALL THE ANCIENT WELSH CLASSICS, THE BATTLE OF THE
Trees, *Cad Goddeu*, is perhaps the one which alludes most
strongly to bardic ideas. It is attributed to Taliesin, who
partook of the extraordinary conflict when Gwydion the
enchanter called up the plants and trees of Britain against
an army of the otherworld generalled by one Peblig the
Strong; and, ultimately, against Arawn[1] King of Annwn.
The encounter is sometimes called The Battle of Achren.

Some say the trees represent alphabetic concepts, perhaps
related, as in Irish ogam,[2] to musical notes, seasonal events
and other correspondences. Some say that the garbled text
we have remaining as the *Cad Goddeu* contains the debris
of druidic ideas regarding sacred groves. It can be guessed
that Celtic druidism, being transmitted orally in the form
of song and story, might also have been transmitted in the
form of the branch of learning here tangled and broken: a
type of tree lore, based on close observation of nature and
containing a philosophic secret and a secret word or name.[3]

In the full text of the *Cad Goddeu* there appear to be
several poems tangled, and several speakers, including
Blodeuwedd,[4] the maiden composed of flowers.

> when plants and trees were sent to war
> warriors against Peblig's power
> the alder tree was at the fore
>
> willow and rowan, tardy both
> plum sharp, starved for death
> briar scarred a host in wrath
>
> bramble's rampart spared no foes
> ivy snared, bean-fostered ghosts
> sea gorse was a source of woes
>
> cherry mocked, birch armed late
> a foreign tree wore foreign shape
> fir was foremost, royal by right

Blodeuwedd (blod éh weth)

before kings, ash took the field
loyal elm would never yield
hazel there for war was steeled

hedge plants fought like bulls of battle
green holly showed its mettle
hawthorn was not gentle

fern and broom, trodden and plundered
mannerless gorse made foe surrender
heather, a handful, pursuing a hundred

mighty oak, doom's door
heaven and earth before him cower
but chestnut shamed the princely fir

Now this battle is said to have been fought to obtain three creatures from the otherworld, the dog, the roebuck and the lapwing. The dog is the guardian of the secret. The roebuck hides the secret, and the lapwing disguises the secret.

dark of darkness, levelled craigs
fire of wood, force of wave
it was then the Great Shout was made

There were arrayed in the ranks of Arawn formidable opponents, and of these, one was invincible as long as his name remained secret. It was Gwydion who guessed it. And he spoke these words:

sure-hoofed my spurred horse
on your shield alder sprigs
Brân is your name, Brân[5] of the branches

sure-hoofed my horse of war
in your hand are sprigs of alder
Brân you are, by the branch you bear

It was thus the battle was won by Gwydion and the forces of the trees.

tips of beech sprout anew
green again whatever grew
and oaks from the Gorchan of
    Maelderw[6]

But regarding the secret kept by the dog, the roebuck
and the lapwing, it is said in the Triads:

three primary essentials of genius
an eye that can see nature
a heart that can feel nature
and a boldness that dares follow it

And it is said that whoever spends the night alone on the
top of Cader Idris[7] or under the Rock of Arddu on the
Llanberis side of Snowdon will be found in the morning dead,
mad, or a poet. It is further said that whoever would be a poet
must take up harp and sorrow and the wandering road.   79

Original text, *Kat Godeu*;
Welsh, c. twelfth century

Maelderw (myle déroo)

THE DIALOGUE
OF THE TWO SAGES

IN ANCIENT IRELAND POETS WERE GRADED, AS WERE THE
bards of Britain, according to degree of mastery in lore and
magic. The Irish poets were called 'fili' and the title of a
master poet was 'ollamh'.

The following piece, an example of bardic interchange,
derives from the twelfth-century Book of Leinster.

About the time of Christ, when the king of Ulster was
Conchobhar mac Nessa, Adna the Ollamh of Ulster died.
His place was bestowed on the poet Fercheirtne, whose
experience and mastery made him a more than likely
candidate. But Adna's son Néde, being away to study in
Scotland and unaware of Fercheirtne's appointment, learned
of his father's death from the sound of the sea waves as he
strolled the shore. He returned at once to Emhain Macha,[1]
capital town of Ulster, to take his father's place.

The first man he met on entering the halls of
Conchobhar was Bricriu,[2] a man who loved to stir up
conflict whenever he could. Bricriu undertook to bestow
the ollamh position on Néde, accepting in return a valuable
gift, remarking only that Néde as a beardless youth was
hardly suitable. Néde plucked a tuft of grass and, uttering a
verse of power, placed it against his chin, where it at once
took on the appearance of a luxuriant beard. And Néde
seated himself in the ollamh seat and about him he wrapped
the robe of three colours: the middle part of it many bright
feathers of birds, the lower part of it white bronze in colour,
the upper part of it bright gold.

Now chuckling to himself, Bricriu set out to tell
Fercheirtne how Néde had stolen his ollamhship, and
Fercheirtne, in a fury, set out for Conchobhar's palace to
deal with the interloper. But when he beheld the youth who
sat in his chair, Fercheirtne was taken aback by his poise,
and addressed Néde with some civility stating, however,

Ollamh (ollav)   Fercheirtne (férkhertuya)
Néde (ney they)   Emhain Macha (évin mákha)   Bricriu (brick ree oo)

that he was occupying the chair awarded to Fercheirtne. Néde replied with equal politeness and formality pointing out Bricriu's malicious jest, but nevertheless requesting that Fercheirtne should satisfy himself that the boy who had unwittingly usurped an already given position was, in fact, most worthy to be Ollamh of Ulster. In establishing this, Fercheirtne addressed Néde thus, as the bards relate:

a question, oh child of education
where do you come from?

to which Néde replied
not hard to answer
from a wise man's heel
from a confluence of wisdoms
from perfection of goodness
from brightness of sunrise
from poetry's hazels
from splendour's circuits
from that state where truth's worth is measured
from that measure where truth is realised
from that reality where lies are vanquished
from where all colours are seen
from where all art is reborn

and you, my elder, where do you come from?
to which Fercheirtne replied
not hard to answer
from the width of the pillars of the age
from the fill of the rivers of Leinster
from the length of the hall of the wife of Nechtan[3]
from the reach of the arm of the wife of Núadu[4]
from the extent of the country of the sun
from the height of the mansions of the moon
from the stretch of a babe's umbilical cord

a question, oh youth of instruction
what is your name?

to which Néde replied
not hard to answer
minuscule and muckle I am
dazzling and highly hard
entitle me Fire's flame
name me Fire of Word
or Noise of Knowingness
or Fountain of Riches
or Sword of Canticles
or Ardent Verity of Genius

and you, my elder, what is your name?

to which Fercheirtne replied
not hard to answer
of seers most sure
I am chief revealer

of that which is uttered
and that which is asked
Inquiry of the Curious
Weft of Deftness
Creel of Verse am I
and Abundance of the Sea

a question, oh young man of learning
what art do you practice?

to which Néde replied
not hard to answer
I bring blush to face
and spirit to flesh
I practice fear's erasure
and tumescence of impudence
metre's nurture
honour's venture
and wisdom's wooing
I shape beauty to human mouths
give wings to insight
I make naked the word

in small space I have foregathered
the cattle of cognisance
the stream of science
the totality of teaching
the captivation of kings
and the legacy of legend

THE VISION OF MAC CONGLINNE

Three men of equal rank—
A king, a harper and a bard
old Welsh proverb

IT HAPPENED LONG SINCE IN ERIN THAT CATHAL KING OF Munster was living the years of his reign afflicted with a terrible thirst and hunger. No amount of gorging would sate his unnatural craving for comestibles and potations. Every known healer was tried for remedy, without success, till there volunteered to the rescue of his country the poet Mac Conglinne.

Now Mac Conglinne came before the king while the king was at his supper. And Mac Conglinne came before the king chewing and grinding his own teeth upon a grindstone. Well, the king paused for a moment, paused from the cramming of the royal cheeks with multiple surfeits of the fruits of earth and water like the ruination of the nation that he was, and he demanded of the poet some explanation of this strange conduct.

And Mac Conglinne said, 'I grieve to see you eat alone!'

This so shamed the king that he tossed the poet some scraps from the royal table, the first act of such humanity seen from him in years.

'Grant me one further boon,' said the poet Mac Conglinne.

'It is granted,' said Cathal king of Munster.

'Fast with me till morning.'

Well the king, though horror stricken, had to comply. He'd given his royal word you see, but he was mad with raging hunger by the first light of day.

It was then that Mac Conglinne ordered the fires to be kindled and the cooks to be cooking. He ordered the largest and most sumptuous of breakfasts. He ordered that ropes and cords and shackles and manacles and chains be brought to bind the king. And the king was bound with knots enough to lace an eel. And Mac Conglinne, taking some

Cathal (ka hal)   Mac Conglinne (ma kon gléen ya)

succulent morsel, was dipping it in honey or sauces and waving it gently backwards and forwards under the king's nose, was popping it into his own mouth while the king got none.

Cathal of Munster writhed and roared in his bonds for his guards to loose him and to kill Mac Conglinne. These requests were not granted to him at this time. And all the while passing delectables before the king's face and into his own Mac Conglinne was reciting these following words, as the bards relate:

a voice in a vision once bid me go seek
on an isle I could see in a vast lake of milk
on whose shores I stood by a sweet little hut
that was thatched all with butter

thatch rods to the roof little puddings they were
of very stiff custards the posts of the door
each bed and bedstead of bacon

and walls of cheese without and within
and sausage beams had this nourishing home
and the voice in my vision said 'rise, poor man
you have the power of guzzling in you
seek doctoring in yonder isle for your sad lack of appetite'

moored in a cove of the lake I found
a little boat of beef boards
curd thwarts it had, its prow was lard
of golden butter its stern was made
with joints of deer meat for its oars
across the lake of milk I steered
through seas of soup and firths of meat
breasting waves of buttermilk
lapped by ripples of flavourful drip
by cheese isles and crowdie shoals
till I came to the plain
twixt Butter Hill and Milk Lake
in the Land of Dawn Gobble
to the dwelling place of the doctor I sought

oh what a house had this wise doctor
staked all about with bacon steaks
and fended with fences of hard lard

unbolting to me the sausage bolt
the keeper came to the gate of cream
Baconboy, son of Butterlet and Lardon
with his comfy brogues of old bacon
his leggings of boiled meat on him
his jerkin of corned beef on him
his belt of salmon hide on him
and his hood of porridge

his horse of salt pork under him
its legs egg custard under it
its oat cake hooves under them
its curd ears, its honey eyes

this lad held a whip with a lash of white puddings
every drop of juice from them
a good man's meal

I could see the doctor I sought within
in his rumpsteak gloves about the house
all hung with tapestries of tripe
and his son in the kitchen, angling with skill
in a deep pool of delightful whey
his hook of lard on a line of marrow
caught whiles a ham or a bit of beef

I entered and spied a couch of butter
where I sat and sank to my hair tips
eight men it took to haul me out

brought to the doctor then, I told him
I yearned to eat
but could not get food

'alack and alas,' said he to me
'sore and dire affliction is this
but I have the cure

in your own hearth kindle a fire of oak
and cook for yourself thrice nine bannocks
of eight grains made, be sure
of wheat and oats and rye and barley
eight flavourings with them
and eight sauces
and when they are ready to be ate
take up a little thimble of drink
only as much as would quench a score
but let it be of golden, gurgling
frothy, foaming
creamy, cooling
refreshing, relishful
sweet white milk

this will cure you

go now in the name of Cheese
and may Bacon guard you
and Yellow Creamy Thick Cream preserve you
and the Mighty Cauldron of Soup watch over you'

Now as Mac Conglinne was saying these words and tempting and teasing the king with food morsels, the demon imp of hunger that possessed and afflicted poor Cathal king of Munster, showed its dark sleek face in the king's gaping mouth. And trying as it was to reach the food, stretched and craned out further . . . and further . . . and further . . . till it fell with a yell into the heart of the fire and the king was cured.

This story was first written down in the twelfth century in Erin; and this is an end of it.

WEE JACK AND THE OLD KING

IN THE DAYS WHEN MUSIC WAS SWEETER AND FIRE WAS hotter and ice was colder and drink was stronger than it is now, the king of Scotland was in his age and weakness and without a child to be his heir. So he decreed that this proclamation be proclaimed at every pulpit, market cross, crossroads and tavern door in all the lands of Scotland, and at every high gate, low gate, hunt gathering, ram sale and occasion of races. And this was the gist of it:

'Whatsoever person, notwithstanding, hereinafter called the *Claimant*, shall induce His Royal Majesty, Our King, to declare said Claimant an Articulator of Subreption, Pseudologia or Improbity, said Claimant shall be deemed Successor, Inheritor and from that day forth, Sole Reigning Monarch of this Domain, its Islands and Near Seas, King under God, until his Natural Term.'

Whoever could make the king call him a liar, do you see, would be crowned king after him.

Well people came from far and near with their oddest tales and extravagances. But the king received all with an impassive gravity, and would pretend to accept as the truth even the most preposterous. Every tale he heard was as good as gospel to him. Or so he would say, while promptly proceeding to order the execution of the misfortunate hopeful before him.

At last word reached Wee Jack himself and Wee Jack determined to try his luck. And Wee Jack set off for the king's castle, dressed up to the nines—one shoe off, one shoe on, the tail of his shirt dangling out of a big hole in the seat of his britches, and an old scythe blade tied round his waist with baling string by way of a sword. Wee Jack sauntered up to the castle gate smiling like all Halloween let loose, and the guards showed him in to the king at once, because everybody was to get a try.

'Ah, come in, come in, Jack,' said the king. 'I'm sorry you've come, for I've no wish to be the death of you. I knew your father well.'

'Oh I never had a father,' said Wee Jack. 'But six years before I was born I was called to be the Salvation of Scotland that time there was the big famine.'

'Before you were born?' said the king.

'That's it,' said Wee Jack. 'Are you calling me a liar?'

'Oh no,' said the king.

'Well,' said Wee Jack. 'Before I was born I came to Edinburgh with a pocket full of sand to help relieve the famine of the people. But even the finest sand would not content them. So I jumped up in the air and landed in Africa. The first man I met there was the king of the Africans, on his hands and knees up a tree in a cave, and he spoke to me in fine words of the Gaelic tongue.'

'He spoke to you in Gaelic?' said the king.

'Yes,' said Wee Jack. 'Are you calling me a liar?'

'No,' said the king.

'Well,' said Wee Jack. 'When the high king of the Africans heard of the famine that was on the Scottish nation, he jumped out of the tree, and landed upon his elbow, spinning like a top. 'Jack,' says he, 'what can I do to aid you?' 'I only need the lend of five hundred thousand tons of barley, wheat, oats and pease meal,' I said. 'Whatever you say yourself,' said the king of the Africans, spinning all the while like a teetotum,[1] and he sent his servants to fetch it from the bottom of the river, where they kept it stored for fear of mildew. They had it all piled up in front of me in no time at all, but I had no bag to carry it, no basket, nothing of that sort. Till I felt a biting at the back of my neck. It was a flea. I grabbed it by its long nose. I stabbed it to death with my thumb. I turned it inside out and crammed the five hundred thousand tons of barley, wheat, oats and pease meal into its gizzard, lungs, belly and lower gut, four grand separate compartments. And I slung the whole lot up on my shoulder in that fine bag of flea-skin.'

'You slung five hundred thousand tons of grain and

meal up on your shoulder in a flea-skin bag?' said the king.

'That's right. Are you calling me a liar?'

'Not you,' said the king. 'Not me,' said the king. 'Not the ghost of a lie in your body, Jack.'

'Well,' said Wee Jack. 'I had the bag up on my shoulder and I jumped up in the air to return to Scotland. But what with the extra weight I couldn't get more than five or six thousand feet up, and I was worrying about the traaa. . .jectory bringing me down into the middle of the North Sea when I saw flying towards me a flock of more than a million sea gulls, flying along with their wings interlaced, and I landed in the middle of that beautiful flying carpet and they carried me back to Scotland in rare style. Oh but they were a mischievous flock of ocean-goers, so they were. For when they had me near my own place, they parted their wings and dropped me from thousands of feet up in the air.

'Luckily a big rock broke my fall, but I was stuck in it up to my neck, just my head sticking out. I thought "what can I do, what can I do?" Till I remembered this fine sword here,' said Wee Jack, brandishing the scythe blade. 'And I inched it up out of the rock till I was able to saw my own head off, and I sent my head down the road to get help.'

'You sawed off your own head,' said the king, 'and sent it off to get help?'

'That's right,' said Wee Jack. 'Are you calling me a liar?'

'Oh no,' said the king. 'Not really.'

'Well,' said Wee Jack. 'My head was bounding along the road when up came this fox, grabbed my head and made off with it. That was the limit of my patience. I was furious. I cracked the rock to flinders and I chased that fox, past Inchkeith, Inchcolm, Inchmickery and Inchgarvie and up the high and low mountains of Yarrow till I caught up with him. I took my head back. I kicked six young foxes out of that fox. Oh he got little cheer meeting with me. And he said to me with his last dying gasp: 'The worst scrap of scrag end and marrow bone butt that ever a poor fox was forced to store till the mould on it went black and the winter froze it into blisters and leather and the worse puddle of owl vomit that ever a starving fox turned up his tail at was better than you, Jack. And the same goes for your bottle-faced, snell-gabbit, mash-witted, bow-backit, dangle-bellied, cack-handed, snibbert and slaistery old pauchle of a king.'[2]

'You're a liar!' said the king, and fell down dead.

And that's the way Wee Jack got the crown.

THE LAD WITH THE GOATSKIN

THERE WAS AN OLD WOMAN ONCE, SO POOR SHE HAD NO clothes to put on her wee boy. So she kept him in the ashpit next to the fire. That kept him warm.

One day as she was hobbling home cursing her bunions, she saw by the road an old goatskin. She thought it would be just the thing for her boy to wear. She took it home for him. She said to him:

'Jimmy, up out of the ashes and get this tucked around ye, son.'

He stood up and he was huge. All that mineral nourishment from the ashes. The magnesium, the aluminium, the selenium, and the zinc. She peered up at him:

'Crivens! Look at the size of ye. Sitting there in the ashes a' these years and never lifting a finger to help me. Away to the woods and bring us back a bit kindling.'

Soon as he started gathering the sticks, out there came a twenty-five foot giant swinging half a tree at him, and roaring, as giants do, 'Hee Haw Hogaraich', and 'Fee Fi Fo Fum' and other things not polite to repeat. Now this half-tree was the giant's magic shillelagh. There was a big iron spike through the end of it. And on that spike a yellow flea. That gave it power.

But the Lad with the Goatskin had spent a lifetime dodging things his mother meant to toss in the fire, so he had no trouble ducking the giant's blow. The giant's club swung around and caught him on the back of his own head. Knocked him to the ground. Made mince-meat of him. The Lad with the Goatskin stamped his foot on the giant's neck.

'What will you give me if I spare your life?'

And the giant answered:

'Aw, please don't kill me. I'll give you me magic shillelagh. It's a fine, solid club and whoever you hit with it you'll make mince-meat of them whether you've a clear conscience or not.'

'And you'll not mind me gathering sticks?' said the Lad with the Goatskin.

'Take all the sticks you want,' said the giant. And he shuffled off.

The Lad picked up the big bundle of firewood and the magic shillelagh and set off for home. The mother was pleased to get the sticks. But the very next morning she said:

'Away and get sticks, ye lazy gomeril, what's keeping ye from the woods?'

He was just getting a good stack gathered when out trundled another giant, two heads he had, one with a leering squint, one with a squinting leer. The Lad with the Goatskin up with the shillelagh, gave him left and right, knocked him to the ground, made mince-meat of him. And stamping a foot on the nearest neck, he roared:

'What will you give me if I spare your life?'

'Oh-h-h, spare me . . . spare me. And I'll give you me feadan . . . me feadan. It's a species of whistle . . . a penny whistle, as they call it . . . not that it costs a penny now, mind you . . . sure there's no value in money these days at all . . . But this is a magic whistle . . . anyone can play it . . . jigs, reels . . . polkas, it plays both of them . . . whoever hears it dances, willy nilly. They'll dance till you stop playing. O-h-h, let me go now . . . let me go. Don't kill me at all at all . . . at all at all.'

No more trouble from him. The Lad took the feadan, played the Harvest Home hornpipe, and the bundle of sticks danced home with the shillelagh.

The mother was pleased to get the sticks. But the very next morning she said to him:

'Ye muckle gowk! Ye neednae think to sit there like Lord Muck. Away and get kindling.'

He'd barely started this time when up there came gallumphing a beezer of a giant. Och he was mighty, this one. Three heads on him. All shaved on the sides with big

93

pink tufts of hair sticking up in the middle, a torn-off T-shirt saying 'Jesus Shaves' and a tattoo round his belly-button saying 'Handmade in Ireland'.

The Lad with the Goatskin up with the shillelagh, gave the giant a skelp that dropped him in his tracks, made mince-meat out of him. And with a victorious gesture of which he was growing overly fond, the Lad with the Goatskin stamped his foot on the giant's neck:

'What will you give me if I spare your life?'

'Aw, please don't kill me,' whimpered the giant. This one spoke in unison. 'Spare my life and I'll give you my jar of iocshlainte. It's a magical ointment that will heal all wounds, mortal, immortal, civil, financial and military.'

The next day being Sunday, the Lad with the Goatskin went for a walk through the town. With his goatskin kilt and his shillelagh over his shoulder, he was surely the dandy now. Any sniggers he heard he put down to jealousy. There was a wee bird singing on a bush, and the song the wee bird sang was:

'The king will give his daughter's hand in marriage to whoever can make her laugh three times.'

'Oh I'd like the princess's hand,' thought the Lad with the Goatskin. 'I'd like the rest of her as well.'

And away he went singing the old Matt McGinn song:

> 'I wish I could marry a princess
> I'd have the time of my life
> I'd never work another day
> I'd just live off my wife
> I'd wine with her and dine with her
> I'd come at her every cry
> I wish I could marry a princess but
> They're in hell-of-a short supply'

The guards at the gate, seeing this huge ash-smeared, goatskin-kilted lout sauntering towards them with a ten foot club, sunk a half-inch of bayonet in his legs by way of greeting. But the Lad up with his shillelagh and knocked one of the guards into the air to the left of him and the other to the right

iocshlainte (eek lantye)

of him. The king's only daughter, three floors up parting her dimity curtains, saw her father's guards fluttering down again like broken umbrellas. She laughed . . . unpleasant child.

'That's once,' said the Lad with the Goatskin.

They had to make him welcome then. They gave him food and a present of money. He bought himself a tartan shirt and a nice pair of corduroys, but still wore the goatskin draped about him, stylish-like.

There was another suitor in the palace at that time. They called him the Laird of Fushiebridge. He had no reason to like the Lad with the Goatskin.

So the following morning when the king was at his breakfast, the Laird of Fushiebridge said to him, privily: 'Mind yon wolf up in the mountains? Ken yon muckle big yin? That's eatin' a' your cows and that? Why don't you get that Jimmy, whatever his name is, with his goatskin, to go and get ye the wolf? That'll settle his barry.'

The king said, 'Ah, wa, wa, wa, awfully good idea. Ga, ga, ga, ga, glad I thought of it. You there, Goatskin Chappie, nip up to the mountains and bring us down the big wolf. The one that's been eating all our sheep. If you can bring us the wolf, then we shall see what we shall see what we shall see. Absolutely, ah.'

High in the mountains. The wolf's lair. Out lolloped the wolf, the biggest ever seen, a yard and a half of tongue and not wagging its tail.

The Lad with the Goatskin whipped out the feadan and commenced to play 'Follow Me Up To Carlow!' The wolf reared up on his hind legs, capering and twirling, and away down the hill went the Lad with the wolf dancing behind him, beside him and around the front of him, jigging for all it was worth.

People they passed heard the music. They began to dance. The Laird of Fushiebridge heard the music. And he began to dance, ochy, ochy, ochy! And the king began to dance, fa fa fa fol de rol de rol de rolly!

The princess was pleating herself, creasing herself

laughing at her father's antics. 'Nothing so funny as daddy!' she was shrieking.

'That's twice,' said the Lad with the Goatskin, and danced the wolf down to the harbour, where they put it on a ship to America. And that's why there's wolves there to this day, you know.

The king was furious, outraged at being made to dance like that. He was burning the midnight oil you may be sure, trying to come up with the ultimate solution to the Goatskin Problem. All of a sudden the answer dawned on him. He sent for the Lad with the Goatskin.

'Ay, ay, ay, ay I want you to go to Hell. Absolutely, ah. Bring me back the Flail of Hell. Sure to be useful for something in statecraft.'

The Lad with the Goatskin set off for Hell. Very easy to find. A moving staircase rolling down and down into the very bowels of the earth. There were the gates of Hell, five hundred miles high and made of showers, cascades and molten streams of silver, scarlet and luminous orange molten lava and boiling metal with wee black imps hopping in and out, squeaking, 'One drop more won't hurt you,' and so on.

The Lad with the Goatskin uncorked his jar of iocshlainte and, spreading some on his hands, flung wide the gates of Hell and strode in, immune. Straight ahead he could see the Devil's house. And through the Devil's door he went without knocking.

The Devil said: 'Sacre bleu! Why are you here?' The Lad explained he'd come to get the Flail of Hell.

The Devil said: 'But I do not wish to give you zis magical weapon.'

The Lad with the Goatskin started in with his shillelagh, smashing the Devil's Louis Quatorze furniture, smashing up the portraits of the Devil's favourite politicians. He was making a hell out of Hell.

And the Devil, pulling himself up his full five feet in his cloven-toed protected species boots, screamed: 'Take zis

Flail, but nevair come 'ere again, you . . . animal!'

Back near the king's castle, the Lad with the Goatskin put the Flail down for a minute to tie one of his shoelaces. The Laird of Fushiebridge sneaked up and grabbed it, to kill the Lad with the Goatskin. But the Flail was still white hot from the fires of hell. It stuck, skin to the flesh, flesh to the bone, bone to the marrow. The wee bones were coming out of the back of the Laird of Fushiebridge's hand. He was thinking to himself: 'Ouch! That smarts!' It took the Lad with the Goatskin and his jar of iocshlainte to heal him of such a wound as that.

There was nothing for it then. They could see the Lad with the Goatskin was set on marrying the princess. She laughed all the way to the church.

They gave them a wedding then, right enough. I was there myself, playing the harp for them. The presents I was given? Butter on a red hot coal and soup in a basket.

How the Lad with the Goatskin got on in his marriage, that's another story.

THE MAN WHO NEVER
DREAMED AT ALL

HARRY THE WEAVER NEVER HAD A DREAM IN HIS LIFE, TILL one night on his way to market he was staying with his friend the tanner.

The tanner said: 'Would you like to have a dream?' Harry said he would very much indeed.

'Well, take these strips of grey sheepskin, tie one of them round one of your hands, tie the other one round the other of your hands, and take this bag of sheep's tallow and tie it to the belt at your waist and go to your bed and go to your sleep. You'll get a dream right enough.'

So Harry tied the one strip of grey sheepskin on the one of his hands, and the other strip of grey sheepskin round the other. He tied the bag of sheep's tallow to the belt at his waist. He went to his bed and to his sleep. He began to dream.

He dreamed it was morning. He dreamed he was up and out on the road to market. But he hadn't gone far on the road to market when he met the son of the king of Clackmannan.

'Good day to you, Harry. Are those gloves you're wearing?'

'No, Your Majesty. These are strips of grey sheepskin I've got tied round my hands, and the reason I am wearing them, Your Majesty, I cannot at this time remember. But I'm on my way to market so.'

'But I want you to deliver this letter for me to Davy Dalrymple, the Blade of Pittenweem.'

'Oh I couldn't do that, Your Majesty. I'd be awful late for market.'

'When I say you must, you must.'

'Oh well, if I must, I must.' Harry took the letter and set off on the road to Pittenweem. But he hadn't gone far on the road to Pittenweem when he happened upon an old woman sitting at her gate. She hadn't walked a step in thirty years.

'Morning, Harry. Are those gloves you're wearing?'

'No, they're strips of grey sheepskin I've got tied round my hands. Why they're there I can't remember now. But I was on my way to market when I met the son of the king of Clackmannan and he commanded me to deliver this letter to Davy Dalrymple, the Blade of Pittenweem.'

'Aye, but before you do that, you'll need to carry me down to Carlisle to get nine pounds of butter.'

'Oh I couldn't do that.'

'When I say you must, you must.'

'Oh well, if I must, I must.' And Harry picked up the old woman on his back, carried her to Carlisle, bought her nine pounds of butter, carried her back with her butter, and set off again on the road to Pittenweem. But he hadn't gone far on the road to Pittenweem when he met the Fox of Walkerburn.

'Nice to see you, Harry. Are those gloves you're wearing?'

'Well what if they are?'

'I see you're carrying a letter. It's addressed to Davy Dalrymple, the Blade of Pittenweem. How do you know it's not instructions to cut your head off? You can't read, can you?' sniggered the Fox.

'But I can.'

'Can you?'

'Of course I can. Give it here a minute.' The Fox took the letter and opened it up with his long tongue. He was very good at opening letters; he used to work for the post office. He began to read. But he hadn't got much further than 'Dear Davy', when they heard in the distance . . . horns and hounds.

'Tut tut,' said the Fox. 'That'll be the Duke of Buccleuch's Hunt, a most uncivilised rabble. I have no interest in meeting them.' And the Fox ran off.

'Give me back that letter,' said Harry the Weaver.

'Not till I've read what's in it,' said the Fox. And he ran and he ran, and he ran and he ran, and he ran and he ran, and he ran and he ran, all the way to Drumnadrochit and there he vanished down a fox hole.

Harry the Weaver, puffing along after him, was gazing at the fox hole in dismay when he remembered a man near Kelso that kept a fine pair of digging dogs. So he lost no time in making his way back south to Kelso. He knocked on the man's door, and explaining his predicament, asked for the loan of the dogs.

'You'll get them,' grunted the man. 'You'll get them this minute.' But the minute and more like it came and went. The man made no move at all.

'I'm a wee bit pressed for time,' said Harry, 'so if you can bring the dogs round I'll get them back to you before the day is out.'

'You'll get them,' grunted the man, continuing to stare at nothing in particular, while the church bell chimed a quarter. 'You'll get them this minute. As soon as you show me a letter of recommendation from your local magistrate and a testimonial of character from your parish priest, vicar, minister or rabbi.'

So Harry went to the magistrate and got a letter of recommendation, and he had to subscribe to the cricket club to get that. And he went to the parish priest and got a testimonial of character, and he had to subscribe to the church belfry repair fund to get that. And he showed these to the man with the dogs.

'You'll get them,' said the man with the dogs. 'Twenty-five pounds a day, have them back by five or you pay for tomorrow as well. Fifty pound deposit, sign here.'

Harry paid him, took the dogs, and made haste to Drumnadrochit. He put the digging dogs down at the foxhole, and they widened it up a treat. And they dug and they dug, and they dug and they dug, and they dug and they dug, and they dug and they dug away down into the bowels of the earth. Far ahead of them they could see the Fox, still running for all he was worth.

'Give me back that letter!' said Harry the Weaver.

'Not till I've read what's in it,' said the Fox. And he

ran and he ran, and he ran and he ran, and he ran and he ran, and he ran and he ran till he came out the other end of the foxhole. Where was that? Connemara. Scrambling through a wire fence, at last the fox dropped that letter. Harry picked it up. He took the dogs back to the man in Kelso.

'That was quick surely,' said the man. 'I'll get your deposit out of the bank on Monday. I'll post you a cheque.'

Harry delivered the letter to Davy Dalrymple, the Blade of Pittenweem.

'What a charming envelope,' murmured Davy, as he shut the door. 'Whoever can it be from? I wonder why it's all covered in teeth marks.'

Harry rushed off on the road to market. But he hadn't gone far on the road to market when he met a shepherd in a pass between two hills.

'Hallo, Harry!' bawled the shepherd. 'Are those gloves you're wearing?'

'No, they're strips of grey sheepskin tied round my hands, and why they're there I can't remember, but on my way to market I met the son of the king of Clackmannan, he commanded me to deliver a letter to Davy Dalrymple the Blade of Pittenweem, but I hadn't gone far on the road to Pittenweem when I passed an old woman that hadn't walked a step in thirty years, she made me carry her to Carlisle and back with the nine pounds of butter she bought there, then I met the Fox of Walkerburn, who was going to read me the letter, but he got chased away by the Duke's Hunt, he went down a foxhole near Drumnadrochit, I borrowed some digging dogs from a man near Kelso, I had to get letters and testimonials before he'd let me have them, we dug out the fox, chased him into the bowels of the earth and out the other side of the tunnel in Ireland, where he dropped the letter, I took the dogs back, took the letter to Davy Dalrymple the Blade of Pittenweem, who never gave me a word of thanks, and now I'm awful late for market and I mustn't tarry. I'm awful late.'

'Aye, but you'll be later yet,' said the shepherd. 'On one day in every seven years a flood comes down between these hills. Oh! I think I hear it coming now.'

Well the water thundered down like galloping horses. It was about his ankles, it was about his knees, it was about his waist. He scrambled up on a boulder but the water swirled ever fiercer to engulf him. Just when he thought all was lost, he saw, soaring, high above him, an eagle.

'Hallo-o-o, Harry! Are those gloves you're wearing?'

Harry explained.

'Give me that bag of tallow on the belt at your waist,' said the eagle, 'and I'll save you.'

So Harry threw the bag of tallow to the eagle, who snapped it up in his strong beak, and alighting beside him on the boulder, bid Harry climb on between his wings.

Then with Harry the Weaver hanging on for dear life, the eagle flapped mightily aloft, till the counties of East Lothian and Berwickshire were stretched below them like a beautiful green and yellow chequer-board, with Torness Nuclear Power Station right in the middle of it.

But they hadn't gone far when the eagle said: 'Oh, but you're heavy, Harry. You're too heavy. Off you go now, off you go!'

'But I'll fall, but I'll fall,' shrieked Harry, clinging on with every finger and toe he had.

'Aye, then I'll brush you off,' said the eagle. And he flew higher and higher and higher and higher and higher and higher till he came near the roof of the sky. He began banging Harry the Weaver against the roof of the sky.

Above the roof of the sky, in Heaven, two heavenly gentlemen were taking an afternoon stroll.

'What's all that noise?'

'You mean that sort of bumping noise?'

'Yes.'

'I'll take a look, shall I?'

'Yes.' The fatter one tip-toed to the edge. His halo

spun gently behind his silver curls. His mild and puffy features were agleam with holy light. He peered down. 'Oh, that's only Harry the Weaver being bumped against the roof of the sky by an eagle.'

'Oh.' In the distance, celestial choirs could be heard rehearsing for their next engagement, the Judgement Day. 'Poke him off with your stick then!'

'Shall I?'

A gleeful grin spread like butter on the other angel's doughy cheeks. 'Yes.'

So the angel poked Harry off with his stick, and he began to fall and fall and fall and fall. And he fell and he fell and he fell and he fell till he found himself hanging on to the lintel of the door in the tanner's house. And that was enough dreaming for Harry.

THE PIPER'S REVENGE

THERE WAS A PIPER ONCE, MAKING HIS WAY BETWEEN WAKES and christenings. It was the bitter end of a Scottish April, sleet and snow enough to freeze a fox. He had been to a certain farm seeking a night's lodgings, but the surly farmer would have none of him and turned him away again to find what shelter he could in the bleak outby.

It would be a day or so later, as I heard it, he was hirpling along in the teeth of a northeast wind, and passing near that same farm he met with three Irish spalpeens. Now these spalpeens were labourers who travelled from farm to farm with their spades on their shoulders, come over to Scotland to lift potatoes and turnips and such.

The piper and the three spalpeens were going the same road, and they trudged on together. Soon the snow came on again and the wind was blowing it into drifts you could lose a horse in, if you had one to lose. And right in the middle of what was left of the road they stumbled over the snow-shrouded corpse of some misfortunate wayfarer that had keeled over and died from the cold. He was frozen solid.

Well the piper, you see, was lacking any scrap of shoes himself to guard his feet, and he tried to get the dead man's shoes off. They looked about his size. But the shoes were frozen solid on the dead man's feet. So borrowing a spade from one of the spalpeens, he hacked off the dead man's feet with it, shoes and all. And he put the shoes, feet and all, into his pocket. And it was the feet gave him the idea of how he could get revenge on the surly farmer.

He said to the spalpeens: 'We'll away to yon house and seek lodgings, and any money ye make while ye're there, ye'll share it with me.' And he explained his plan to them.

He waited in hiding while the three spalpeens went up to the door. And when the farmer saw these three hulking lads with the spades he didn't like to refuse them commons and lodgings. Oh, he was a stick of a man, a stale crust of a man, a miserly hook of a man, not given to hospitality, but it was three to one, you see. Soon enough, they were sitting by his meagre fire.

In came the farmer's daughter with a bucket of snow to melt for gruel. Now at that time it was the custom to keep the cows in one side of the house while dwelling in the other. It helped to keep the house warm. So while she was melting the snow, she warned them where they were settled:

'Don't sleep near that grey cow at the end, she's gey crabbit, she might bite your jaickets.'

In a wee while, the piper knocked at the door himself, and the farmer, with one squint at the old bundle of rags he'd turned away before, was about to turn him away again.

But if he was, the spalpeens were all chiming in: 'Holy Mary and Sweet Saint Joseph, let your man out of the weather, will yez?' 'Look at the poor soul with no shoe to his foot!' 'He must be a great singer, he has the legs of a thrush.'

So the farmer was forced to display his hospitality twice in the same hour. In shuffled the piper, and the farmer's daughter warned him as he was settling in for the night:

'Don't sleep near the grey cow, she might nibble at your bagpipes,' and she giggled herself up to her attic bedroom, and left them to their gruel.

In the middle of the night, the piper got the dead man's feet out of his jacket pocket and thawed the shoes off them at the fire. And long before the dawn of day he put the dead man's shoes on his own bare feet and slipped quietly out the door and off down the road. He left the dead man's feet where he'd been sleeping, near the grey cow.

In the morning, the farmer's daughter came in with a bucket of snow to melt for porridge and she asked hopefully: 'Does the piper no want his breakfast?'

'Jaysus, I haven't seen hide or hair of him,' said the

gey crabbit: highly irritable

first spalpeen.

'Do you mean the piper that was here last night?' said the second spalpeen.

'Yon poor auld cripple in his last frailty? The last I saw of him, he was sleeping at the far end near the grey cow,' said the third.

The farmer's daughter, glancing over at the grey cow, saw the dead man's feet.

'Merciful powers! What next!' she exclaimed. 'The cow's eaten the piper!'

When the farmer heard of this he came to the spalpeens wringing his hands like hens' necks. 'Here lads, I'll tell ye what's what. Five pounds says it never happened, eh? Och, better make it ten, just haud yer whisht, fifteen, bite yer teeth.'

The spalpeens went off down the road till they met the piper. And they shared the money.

IV

HEROES AND DESTINY

WHEREAS A WIZARD MIGHT SEEK TO OUTWIT DESTINY, THE hero's immortality lies in unflinchingly confronting his own death at the hands of a malevolent fate. Though distinctions between natural and supernatural are not clearly drawn in these tales, otherwise the scene is firmly set in the human world dominated by the aristocratic warrior caste, with their freebooting and thirst for glory.

CONALL CROVI

This is the story of Conall Crovi,[1] a story of fame in the west of Scotland. A story of a time neither mine nor yours, when the King of England's sons went over to France, the three of them, to get learning. When they came home after, they were taking their own time about settling down.

One night they called at the house of Conall Crovi. Whether or not they learnt learning abroad, they learnt no manners, for after getting meat of the best and drink of the full glass, they told Conall Crovi to bring in his maid, his daughter and his wife to attend them with affections. Conall Crovi smiled a crooked smile at that. And as if to go at their bidding went instead, by way of his chambers, out to the stables—his wife, his daughter and his maid with him. They rode away to the King's high hall to seek justice for the insult of the King's three sons.

The King's watcher spied them coming from the blue of the distance, and he told the King Conall Crovi was riding there, and three riders with him.

'Oh, that's the way of things,' said the King. 'Conall Crovi's got my three sons in his power, and he's coming now to make demands of me for their release.'

So the King gave Conall Crovi no hearing at all. Conall Crovi became outlaw from that day, plundering off England's wayfarers till the kingdom was troubled by him from end to end. The King put a steep reward upon the head of Conall Crovi. The King sent his speedy horse rider to find Conall Crovi if he took a year and a day, and after a year and a day the speedy horse rider still had not come near him, till Conall Crovi's own watcher spied the speedy horse rider and took word to Conall Crovi.

'Och well,' said Conall Crovi. 'The poor man is perhaps outlawed as we are ourselves.' And he made the speedy horse rider welcome. He gave him meat of the best, and drink of the full glass and a soft bed after.

By and by, Conall Crovi called to him softly, 'are you

sleeping, speedy horse rider?'

'Not yet!' came the reply.

Soon and again, Conall Crovi called to him softly, 'Are you sleeping, speedy horse rider?'

And the reply came back again, 'Not yet!'

But the third time Conall Crovi called softly to the speedy horse rider there came no reply.

Then Conall Crovi roused the house and his men to arms, for he knew the host of the King's three sons would soon be upon them. And so they were! But Conall Crovi and his men laid on so fiercely they left not a man alive of them but the King's three sons of England.

And Conall Crovi took them, and bound them, straitly, and painfully, with the binding of the three narrows, wrists, ankles and neck.

'Fetch me the sharpening stone,' said Conall Crovi, 'till I get a good edge on my blade. For I am now about a work the like of which I have never done before.'

'What work is that?' said his man who brought the stone.

'Taking the heads off the King's three sons,' said Conall Crovi back to him.

'Don't do it!' said the first son, 'and I'll take your part in right or wrong forever.'

'Don't do it!' said the second son, 'and I'll take your part in right or wrong forever.'

'Don't do it!' said the third son, 'and I'll take your part in right or wrong forever.'

Conall Crovi spared them their lives. Together they rode away to the King's high hall.

The King's watcher spied them coming from the blue of the distance and told the King.

'Oh, so that's the way of things,' said the King. 'Make the doors open for them, then take Conall Crovi and hang him.'

But when they had Conall Crovi up on the gallows, the King's three sons offered their own lives instead of his.

So the King of England put his fate on Conall Crovi, and on his three sons: that they must needs go seek and steal the three black, white-faced stallions of the King of Erin. He put them under crosses and spells that they could not refuse this fate. They took ship, prow to the waves, stern to the land, no mast unbent nor sail untorn till they came to Erin.

In the dark of Erin's night they crept into the stables of Erin's King to steal his black, white-faced stallions. But as soon as they laid the lightest finger on the one of them, such a scream as the stallions raised brought at a run the stallions' guards, and they captured the three sons of the King of England and Conall Crovi where they were hiding, under an old barrel. Captive they were taken before the King of Erin.

The King of Erin took one look at Conall Crovi and said: 'Ach, Conall Crovi, so it's you, ye auld blackguard. I've been after you a while. Now I'll just order the gallows makers to put up a good gallows for you, and we'll get you hung as soon as they're done with it.'

They bound Conall Crovi straitly and painfully with the binding of the three narrows, and they slung him into the dungeon. The King's three sons of England were sent upstairs to take a glass with the King of Erin, and to discuss the question of ransom.

Supper was on the table, fork into meat, tongue into drink, when the King of Erin called for some tale of prodigies and marvels. None there had a tale to tell. They thought then of Conall Crovi. He was brought up and untied to tell them one.

'I'll tell you a tale right enough,' said Conall Crovi. 'If I get the worth of it.'

'Oh you'll get that,' said the King of Erin. 'If it's not your own head spared, or a hair harmed of anyone here.'

'Och well,' said Conall Crovi. 'When I was a boy I was fishing one day in the mouth of the sea. A great ship came sailing by. "Do you know the way to Rome?" so hailed the helmsman to me. "None knows the same better than myself," was the reply I made to him. Although I confess, I did not know where Rome was, any better than I know where the moon goes to bed. I lied to them at that time, and I went on board as the well paid navigator. Every land they reached they would say "is this Rome?" "Not yet!" was the answer they got from me. Till at last, on one great island, where we all went ashore I went off walking and strolling myself alone, and when I returned to the moorings, the ship had sailed without me.

'Cruelly abandoned in a strange land, I did not know what to do, but following my fortune, I came near a house, and there came from it the sound of a woman crying and lamenting. I went in, and asked her the cause of her sorrow. She told me the Lady of the island had died a while back, and they'd been putting off her burial, awaiting the return of her brother, who was away. But they'd be burying her that day. They could wait no longer.

'I went along to the burial of the Lady, and I saw them put down into the grave with her a bag of gold below her head, and a bag of silver below her feet. I thought to myself that I could make better use of that gold and silver than the poor dead woman.

'So I came back that night and opened up the grave. It was only a great stone that covered it. And I let myself down into the dark of the tomb. But I'd no sooner got the money from under her head and feet than bad luck jostled and moved the great stone above me, and down it fell, closing up the grave. And me down there along with the dead woman. Try as I might, I could not shift the stone at all.

'Oh, King of Erin, was I not in a worse plight then than I am tonight, under your mercy, with a hope yet for liberty?'

'Ah, ye auld blackguard,' said the King of Erin. 'You got free of that but you'll not get free of this.'

'Give me the worth of my story,' said Conall Crovi.

'What is it?'' said the King of Erin.

'The eldest son of the King of England to marry your eldest daughter, and one of your black, white-faced stallions as her dowry.'

'You'll get that,' said the King of Erin.

Then they bound Conall Crovi straitly and painfully with the binding of the three narrows. And they slung him back down into the dungeon. And a marriage of twenty days and twenty nights was made for the young couple.

When they were weary of eating and drinking, the King could keep no longer from hearing the rest of Conall Crovi's tale and how he got out from the grave. So they brought Conall Crovi up from the dungeon and into the banqueting hall where they untied him.

'You'll hear my story if I get the worth of it,' said Conall Crovi.

'You'll get that,' said the King of Erin. 'If it's not your own head spared or a hair harmed of anyone here.'

'Och well,' said Conall Crovi. 'I was in the dead dark and silence of the tomb for hours or days till I heard the scrape of crowbars and voices above me. The Lady's brother had at last returned. They opened the tomb. The brother leaned over for one last sight of his sister. And out of the dark I moaned: "oh catch me by the hand and help me out of the tomb!" Well whatever the devil they thought I was they ran as good a clip away as ever I saw men run. And I ran as fast as any.

'I never stopped till I came to the other side of the island, where three young lads were sitting casting of lots. It seemed that a ferocious giant had abducted their lovely sister, and they were sitting and a-casting of lots to decide which of them should go down into the depths of the earth to seek her where the giant had his lair. They cast for me a lot for myself also, and it fell to me to go down and seek the sister.

'They let me down into the earth in a basket tied to a rope. Away down I went, till I came far into the deeps of the earth below, and I saw the beauty of the sweetest girl ever seen winding gold thread on a silver reel, passing the time, so.

'I took her to where the basket was and helped her in, and told her I'd soon settle the giant for her. Up she went. "Send the basket back for me tomorrow" was the request I made of her there, and she swore faithfully she would fulfill it.

'It wasn't long till I heard the giant coming, the thump of his clodhoppers and a string of dead over his shoulder like mackerel. I made haste to hide myself the only place I could find, under a great pile of gold and jewels.

'Surely the giant sought high and low for the lovely girl he'd hoped to see waiting for him there. You would have heard the howl he gave if you were there when she was not. At last he abandoned the search, got a good fire going, gave a wee singe to the bodies he had, and swallowed them all for his supper.

'Now he reached for his pile of gold and jewels, and started counting it over. In that pastime he laid his hand upon my own head.

"So you are the thief of my lovely woman," he roared at me. "I'll polish my teeth on you for my breakfast!"

'He trussed me up and he went to his sleep. But he was unacquainted with the binding of the three narrows. I escaped with little difficulty. I got the spit into the fire red-hot and stabbed it into the middle of his snoring. That kept him, till I grabbed his sword and made a stump of him.

'Soon as I heard the basket let down to fetch me I ran to fill it with jewels and gold from the hoard to help me on my way. When I had the basket filled I climbed in myself, gave the rope a tug and up they began to pull me. But halfway up the rope broke and I fell down and down and down.

'Oh, King of Erin, was I not in a worse plight then than I am tonight, under your mercy with a hope yet for liberty?'

'Ah ye auld blackguard,' said the King of Erin. 'You got free of that but you'll not get free of this.'

'Give me the worth of my story.'

'What is it?'

'The second son of the King of England married to the second of your daughters, and another of your black, white-faced stallions for her dowry.'

'You'll get that,' said the King, and they bound Conall Crovi straitly and painfully with the binding of the three narrows, and slung him back down into the dungeon.

A wedding of twenty days and twenty nights was made for the young couple. When they were weary of eating and drinking, the King could keep no longer from hearing the rest of Conall Crovi's tale, and how he escaped from the giant's cave. So they brought Conall Crovi up from the dungeon and into the banqueting hall and they untied him there.

'You'll hear my story,' said Conall Crovi, 'if I get the worth of it.'

'You'll get that,' said the King of Erin. 'If it's not your own head spared or a hair harmed of anyone here.'

'Och well,' said Conall Crovi. 'I wandered through miles of tunnels till I came out again into the light, near a woman's house, and she standing on her step, a baby in the one of her hands and a big knife in the other. She was lamenting and weeping and these were the words she gave me in explanation and in reply to my inquiry: "Oh sir, I am captive to three giants, and they have ordered my poor baby killed and cooked for flavouring of their evening broth." "That will never be," I told her. "I see three men hanged on yonder gallows. I'll cut one of them down and you can cook up bits of him in place of the babe. I will myself, in order that the giants may know nothing, take the place of the man we steal from the gallows."

'That night, when the giants were slurping their broth, one would say: "This is the fine flesh of a babe," and another would say, "It is not, it is o'er tough and dry like a hanged man's flesh."

'One of them came to the gallows to cut a steak of one of the hanged men's flesh to make comparison. And the first hanging man he came to was myself. And he began to cut a steak out of me.'

Oh, King of Erin, was I not in a worse plight then than I am tonight, under your mercy, with yet a hope of liberty?'

'Ah, ye auld blackguard. You got free of that, but you'll not get free of this.'

'Give me the worth of my story.'

'What is it?'

'The youngest son of the King of England married to your youngest daughter, and the last of your black, white-faced stallions for her dowry.'

'You'll get that,' said the King. And they bound Conall Crovi straitly and painfully with the binding of the three narrows, and slung him back into the dungeon.

For the young couple they made a marriage of twenty days and twenty nights. And when all were weary of eating and drinking, the King could wait no longer in the hanging of Conall Crovi.

But he wanted to hear the rest of the story. So they brought up Conall Crovi and untied him.

'Now, before I hang you,' said the King. 'Tell us how you escaped the time the giant was cutting the steak out of you, and you hanging on the gallows there.'

'Och well,' said Conall Crovi. 'When he was cutting the steak out of me, never a word I spoke. And when the three giants were all asleep, I came down from the gallows and got healing from a magic potion the woman had. The three giants? I killed them all. And I came away.

'I rescued and preserved the woman and the babe. We went together till we found the giants' ship-moorings and took ship and sailed till we reached a land that was not unlike this land of yours. And the woman and the babe, I left them there, among their own.'

Then the old mother of the King of Erin called out

from beside the fire: 'King of Erin, you should do this man honour and free him without delay. For I was that same woman, and you were that babe.'

BRANWEN

LLYR[1] INDEED HAD MANY CHILDREN AS THE SEA
has many waves. All the songs of the world come
whispering and howling out of the craneskin bag of his son
Manannán. Many a sad song among them. One of the
saddest is this following, of Llyr's son Brân and his sister
Branwen.

Blessed Brân[2] son of Llyr was lord of kings in Britain.
It is said he was of such a size that no house could contain
him. He kept court in steep Harlech above the waves, he
and his brother Manawydan,[3] and his mother's two sons
Nissyen and Evnissyen, his half-brothers. Nissyen was a
peace maker by nature, but Evnissyen was a maker of strife,
conflict, discord, argument and malice.

One day, thirteen smooth, high-sailed ships sailed in
from Ireland. Fine ships indeed, with flags of silk.
Messengers sent to meet them learned that these were the
ships of Matholwch King of Ireland, that he sought an
alliance with Brân, and the hand of Brân's sister Branwen.

Brân made them welcome, consultations began,
agreements were made, days set and feasts prepared, and
when those meats were roasted and consumed, and when
that drink was drunk Matholwch slept with Branwen,[4]
Branwen the beautiful.

But as the whole court slumbered, there returned
Evnissyen, enraged that his opinion or consent had not
been sought in the matter of his sister's betrothal. And in
revenge he took sword to Matholwch's horses, wonderful
Irish horses Matholwch had brought with him. Evnissyen's
sword bit their lips to the teeth, lopped their ears to the
head, cropped their tails to the rump, and when he could
get a rope on them he cut their eyelids away, as the bards
relate.

Matholwch's men told him of the maiming of his
horses. 'Lord, you have been disgraced, and this the
Welshmen must have intended.'

Llyr: hleer   Matholwch (math ól ooch)

'Why, if they wished to disgrace me, would they have bestowed on me so fine a maiden as royal Branwen?'

'Lord, your shame is before all the people. You must return to your ships.'

When Brân heard what was happening he sent messengers after Matholwch. 'Offer him a sound horse for every one that has been injured, a silver staff as thick as his little finger and as tall as he stands, and a golden plate as wide as his face.' He urged the messengers to explain what nature of man Evnissyen was.

The messengers presented Brân's words to Matholwch with such skill that he listened to them and returned to hold counsel. But talk as he might, it became plain to Brân that Matholwch did not consider the compensation enough.

'As sure proof of my goodwill to you, I will add to your compensation one of our country's greatest treasures. It is a cauldron,' said Brân, 'and the power of it is this. That a man killed today and thrown into it will rise from it to fight as well tomorrow, save that he will have lost the power of speech.'

This pleased Matholwch, and the following day his full compensation was made over to him. As the kings were talking on the second night, it transpired that Matholwch knew something of the cauldron. He had seen with his own eyes a giant come scrambling with it out of a lake in Ireland, a giant and his wife. Every child this giant woman bore was an armed warrior. They had become such a trouble to the people of Ireland that Matholwch had tried to destroy them by roasting them in an iron house, in which he had made them drunk. But they had escaped, it seemed, and had come to Wales.

After their fill of feasting and the full sweetness of their repose, Matholwch and Branwen sailed away to Ireland. They were welcomed there with great joy. No noble man or lady left Branwen's presence but she gave them a royal gift, a jewel, a brooch, a ring; and so, in her first year there her praises resounded. In course of time she gave birth to a child. They named him Gwern.[5] But in the second year, people began increasingly to grumble at the insult Matholwch had received in Wales, the maiming of his horses, and this grumble became a tumult, and this tumult an outrage and a demand for revenge.

This was the revenge they took. Branwen was driven from her palace rooms and made to cook for the court. The king's butcher came every day when he had finished cutting the meat to give her a box on the ears. The Irish thought that by avoiding all commerce with Wales and by imprisoning all Welshmen coming to Ireland, to keep their ill-treatment of Branwen secret. Three years passed.

Branwen reared a starling in her kitchen, taught it what manner of man her brother was, and sent it with a letter to Wales. It flew swift and sure, alighted on Brân's shoulder, and he learned of his sister's plight. He called together the one hundred and fifty-four districts of Wales and prepared to invade Ireland. Bran himself waded across the sea, his ships beside him.

Matholwch's swineherds were herding their pigs by the shore when they saw the Welsh fleet sailing in, and they rushed to Matholwch: 'Lord, we have seen a forest on the sea and a mountain by the forest, a high ridge on the mountain, and a lake on either side of the ridge, and all moving towards Ireland.' Neither Matholwch nor his advisers could think of anyone to explain this better than Branwen, so they asked her: 'Lady, what is the meaning of this wonder?' She replied 'Though I am no longer a lady of rank among you I will tell you. The forest on the sea is the masts and spars of my brother's ships, the mountain beside the forest is my brother's head as he wades through the sea, the ridge on the mountain is his nose and the two lakes either side of it his eyes.'

Matholwch and his men hastily withdrew to the far side of the River Liffey, destroying the bridge over it as they went. For they had lodestones in the bed of the river they were assured would sink all ships that tried the crossing. But Brân lay down across the Liffey, saying as he did so 'a fo benn byd bont, he who would lead must be a bridge', a saying which has become a proverb in Welsh. His army crossed over his body, and assembled on the far shore. When Brân stood up on the far side, Matholwch's messengers hastened to greet him, saluting him as kinsman and assuring him that Matholwch intended the crown of Ireland on Brân's nephew, Gwern. This was to be as sure recompense for the ill-treatment of Branwen. Peace talks were begun at Branwen's own request. She had no wish to see Ireland laid waste.

The Irish set themselves to build a house large enough even for Brân, in which the peace talks and feasting might take place. But of this house they made a trap. It had a hundred pillars, on every pillar a peg, on every peg a leather bag, in every leather bag an armed man.

Evnissyen entered the house in advance of the Welsh army and scanned the huge hall with a warrior's gaze: 'What's in this bag, friend?' he asked an Irish servant who was laying the tables. 'Flour, friend. Only flour.' Evnissyen put his hand into the neck of the bag until he found the warrior's head, and he squeezed it till he felt his fingers crush the skull and enter the brain. 'And what's in this bag, friend?' he asked again, pointing to the next one. 'Flour, friend,' replied the Irishman. And Evnissyen served the warrior in that bag as he had the first, until he had killed them all, singing at the end of this work the following englyn (verse), as the bards relate:

> These bags now hold a flour well milled
> armed men thick as sheaves
> warriors prepared to kill

The peace talks then went ahead unhindered, and feasting around a great fire, and at the conclusion of the feast Gwern was invested with the kingship of Ireland. Brân called the boy over to him, and he went gladly, and from

Brân to Manawydan, and from Manawydan to Nissyen. Everyone who saw the boy loved him. Evnissyen called, 'Why does not my nephew, the son of my sister, come to me?' When Gwern went over to him, Evnissyen rose suddenly taking Gwern by the feet. And before anyone could stop him he hurled the boy headfirst into the blazing fire. At once everyone in the house sprang to arms, Brân protecting his sister between his shield and his shoulder and preventing her from leaping into the flames after her son. Deaths were given and taken and the battle raged unceasingly for days and nights. But the Irish brought out the Cauldron of Rebirth and their dead thrown in soon rose again as fierce as ever.

At last it was Evnissyen who crept in among the Irish dead and was thrown into the cauldron among them. He stretched out inside it till the cauldron broke in four pieces. His heart broke also. Such victory as there was then went to Brân. Little victory. Only seven of his men and Branwen survived. He himself was wounded in the foot with a poisoned spear. The names of those who lived were Pryderi, Manawydan, Glinyeu eil Taran, Taliesin, Ynawg, Gruddyeu son of Muryel, and Heilyn son of Gwynn Hen.

Brân requested his companions to cut off his head and carry it with them as they returned to Britain. He said to them: 'you will spend seven years feasting at Harlech with the Birds of Rhiannon⁶ singing to you. My head will be as good a companion to you as ever I was when fully alive. After that you will spend eighty years at Gwales in Pembrokeshire. There will be several doors in the house. As long as you do not open the door that faces Cornwall, your sorrow will be kept from you and the head will not decay. But if once you up and open that door, you must set out at once and bury the head on the White Hill in London, with its face towards France.'

So they cut off Brân's head and crossed the sea to Anglesey. Branwen looked back at Ireland and forward at Britain, and weeping that two islands had been brought to war and disaster on her account, her heart broke, and they made her a four-sided grave on the banks of the River Alaw.

The seven survivors journeyed on, carrying Brân's head, through a Britain now ruled by the usurper Caswallawn son of Beli. And at length they came to Harlech, where the three magic Birds of Rhiannon sang them a music of peace in war, of war in peace, and of the freedom of the heart from bondage. Seven years passed, and they went to Gwales, where they found a great royal hall overlooking the sea. There were three doors, two open and one closed, the one that faced Cornwall. The eighty years they spent there in joyful conversation with the head of Brân were as if no time passed. This assembly was called the Assembly of the Wonderful Head. But one day Heilyn son of Gwynn Hen decided to test the truth of the prophecy regarding the door facing Cornwall. He opened it. All the grief that had befallen them swept over them again like a flood. They took the head and set out at once for London, and they buried the head on the White Hill in London. This burial the bards have recorded as one of the 'Three Happy Concealments' and one of the 'Three Unhappy Disclosures' when it was unburied. For while the head lay there, no plague came across the sea to the island of Britain.

In Ireland meanwhile no man was left alive. Only five pregnant women in a cave in the wilds. These women all bore sons at the same time, and when each grew he took to wife another's mother. And they lived in the land and divided it in five among them, for which reason the parts of Ireland are still called 'fifths'. They scoured Ireland wherever there had been battles and there found gold and silver and became rich. So ends this Branch of the *Mabinogion*.

from the original Welsh text,
c. eleventh century

LLEU

THE STORY OF LLEU[1] IS ONE OF THE GREATEST
Classics of Celtic mythology. Oddly humorous, oddly
brutal, oddly unfair and tantalisingly allusive to ancient
lore now obscure.

Math son of Mathonwy was lord of North Wales, while
Pryderi son of Pwyll[2] was lord of the South. Math was a
great wizard, whatever words or whispers were voiced in
the air he would know of them, but his life could only be
maintained if his feet were resting in the lap of a virgin.
Unless he was at war. The virgin who held his feet in her
lap was named Goewin.

Math's nephews were at his court in these times: their
names were Gilfaethwy[3] son of Dôn and Gwydion son of
Dôn, and Gilfaethwy became obsessed with a passion for
Goewin. She haunted his thoughts night and day till he
grew sick with love for her. Gwydion said to him, 'Brother,
say nothing to me, lest the wind carry words amiss. I know
what troubles you, and I will hatch a plan for you.'

They went to Math. Gwydion told him of a new kind
of animals in the world. Animals that had come from
Annwn as a gift to Pwyll, and that these pigs as they were
called, were in the keeping of Pwyll's son Pryderi, in the
South. He mentioned that the taste of their meat was far
better than beef. Math was not slow in agreeing to let his
nephews see if they could get some of them.

So they set off to meet with Pryderi disguised as bards,
for Gwydion was the greatest story-teller in the world. And
having charmed Pryderi with his accomplished tongue, he
offered for the pigs twelve steeds, gold-saddled, gold-
bridled, twelve black white-breasted hunting dogs, with
gilded collars and gilded leashes and twelve golden shields.
This offer Pryderi accepted.

Gwydion and Gilfaethwy left hastily with the pigs.
The steeds and dogs and shields were all made by

Lleu (hleye)   Goewin (goywin)   Gilfaethwy (gil vye thwee)

Gwydion's spells out of toadstools and mushrooms. They could not be expected to last.

The brothers arrived back at Math's fortress, Caer Dathyl, with the whole of the South up in arms behind them. Math marshalled his forces. He rode off to join battle, leaving Goewin to the mercy of Gilfaethwy, who lay with her that night against her will.

The following morning, Gwydion and Gilfaethwy rode to join their uncle's army, and in the thick of the battle a combat was set aside for Gwydion and Pryderi. By strength with the aid of magic, Gwydion killed Pryderi in that fight.

The South returned to their land with lamentations, and in the midst of the celebrations of the North Math called for Goewin, that he might again place his feet in her lap as his destiny required.

'Lord,' said Goewin, 'seek a virgin who may sit with your feet in your lap, for Gilfaethwy your nephew has raped me and shamed you. Nor was I silent. There can have been no one in the house who did not hear my cries. Gilfaethwy and Gwydion are the cause of my dishonour.'

Math took Goewin by the hand and said to her, 'As far as I can, I will do right by you. I will make you my wedded wife and queen of my kingdom.'

Meanwhile, the whereabouts of Gwydion and Gilfaethwy could not be ascertained. Only when Math made them outlaw, with a prohibition on all his people to give them food or shelter did they at last show themselves in his court again. They set themselves at his will.

'If it were at my will,' said Math, 'I would not have lost so many good men in battle, I would not have wished Pryderi's death, I would not have wished Goewin shamed as she has been.'

Math struck Gilfaethwy with his magic staff, and Gilfaethwy became a hind. And Math struck Gwydion and Gwydion became a stag. And Math said, 'Since you will mate in the manner of wild beasts, let this be your destiny.'

At the end of a year, the stag and the hind returned to

Caer Dathyl, and a young deer with them. Math struck them again with his staff. One became a sow, one became a boar, and the young deer became a fine boy. Math named him Hyddwn son of the Deer.

A year from that day the sow and the boar came back to Caer Cathyl, and a young pig with them. Math struck them again with his staff. One became a wolf, one became a wolf bitch, and the young pig became a fine boy. Math named him Hychdwn   son of the Pig.

A year from that day the wolf and the wolf bitch came back to Caer Dathyl, and a young wolf with them. Math struck the young wolf with his staff, and he became a fine boy. Math named him Bleiddwn son of the Wolf. He struck the other two and Gwydion and Gilfaethwy stood before him in their own shapes once more.

'Nephews,' said Math, 'you have harmed me and I have punished you, and you have had great shame, bearing children to each other. Now you have got peace and we shall have friendship. Give me advice as to what virgin I should choose to hold my feet in her lap.'

'Lord,' said Gwydion. 'It is not hard for me to advise you. Choose my sister Arianrhod[4] daughter of Dôn, your sister's daughter.'

So Arianrhod was sent for. 'Are you a virgin, Arianrhod?' asked Math.

'As far as I know I am,' said Arianrhod.

Math held out his magic staff so that it was a few inches off the floor. 'Step over this staff,' he said, 'and if you are a virgin I will know it for certain.'

She stepped confidently over the magic staff, but as she did so there fell from her womb a big, yellow-haired boy. This boy began to utter cries. Loud, piercing, insistent. Arianrhod ran for the door, but as she did she dropped another little tiny something, which Gwydion, in the confusion, deftly whisked away. He wrapped it in silk and hid it in a magic casket he kept by his bedfoot.

As for the big fair-headed boy, Math gave him the

Hyddwn (huh thoon)   Hychdwn (huhch doon)   Bleiddwn (blaythoon) name Dylan. And as soon as he was named he ran till he reached the shore of the sea, and wading into the sea he took the character of the sea. He swam away at once. For this the bards have titled him Dylan Eil Ton, Twin of the Wave.

In due time there formed within Gwydion's magic casket, as he had expected, another baby boy, and Gwydion took this babe to town where there was a woman to suckle him. When the boy was a year old he was as big as a two-year-old. When he was two he was able to return to Caer Dathyl on his own. At Caer Dathyl Gwydion set himself to foster him.

By the time the boy was four he would be taken for a sturdy eight-year-old, and one day Gwydion took him over the hills to Arianrhod's Court, Caer Arianrhod.

Gwydion greeted Arianrhod pleasantly, warmly, with a 'God prosper you'. But, 'Who is that boy with you?' was all the greeting he got back from her.

'He is your son,' said Gwydion.

Arianrhod paled with rage, hissing, 'What gives you the right to shame me by keeping him like this?'

'It is small shame to foster a boy as fine as this.'

'What is your boy's name?'

'He has no name yet.'

'Well,' said Arianrhod, 'this curse I will put on him. He will get no name till he gets one from me!'

They parted angrily. Gwydion and the boy returned to Caer Dathyl. Next morning they set off along the shore gathering coarse seaweed and dulse as they went. Of the coarse seaweed, Gwydion made by his enchantments a magic ship, of the dulse, he made a quantity of fine shoe-leather. He gave them each the seemingness of shoemakers, and in this guise they sailed into the port of Caer Arianrhod.

Arianrhod, of course, learning there were fine shoemakers at her gate, sent down her servant with her foot measurements to order shoes. But Gwydion sent her first a size far too big, next a size far too small, and finally sent word that he could not make shoes for her till he could see her foot for himself.

Now Arianrhod was not over-willing to be displaying her noble foot to a common tradesman, but such wonderful shoes as she had already seen were too much to resist. She came to the dockside. 'God prosper you, shoemakers,' was the greeting she gave to them. 'I am astounded you can not make shoes from measurements.'

'Ah, your Ladyship,' said Gwydion, kneeling before her and taking her foot in his two hands. 'I could not before but I can now.'

It was at that moment a wren[5] perched on the top mast of the ship. The boy threw a stone at it striking the wren's leg between the tendon and the bone, as the bards relate.

Arianrhod smiled slightly. 'A sure hand has the fair-haired boy.'

'Well,' said Gwydion. 'Since you name him so, Lleu Llaw Gyffes he shall be called (Fair-Haired One with the Skilled Hand).' The shoe on her foot turned to wet brown bladderwrack, all the fine leather was seaweed again, the ship and the fittings with it, and Gwydion and Lleu stood before her in their own shapes.

Arianrhod stabbed at the air with a quivering finger. 'This curse I put on the boy,' she shrieked. 'He shall never get arms till I arm him myself!'

This was a terrible curse in those days, for a noble youth could not attain honourable manhood without winning the right to bear arms. But by another of his sly tricks, Gwydion deceived Arianrhod into giving Lleu arms, and this before a hand of years had passed. It was then Arianrhod put her final and most venomous curse on Lleu. That he might never marry a wife of any race in the world.

This stumped even Gwydion. He was forced to consult with his uncle, Math. And Math suggested that they fashion for Lleu a wife made of flowers. They made their incantations. And it was of meadowsweet and maythorn they made her and of the flowers of chestnut, nettle, blue cornflower, broom, oak buds, red bean flower and the sweet primrose of spring. This maiden they made was as beautiful as the daylight. Lleu loved her passionately as soon as he set eyes on her. Blodeuwedd was the name they gave her, which means Flower Face.

They were soon married and set up court very happily in lands Math gave them. People and land flourished under the rule of Lleu.

But as fate would bend the story, despite the work of wizards, it befell at a time while Lleu was away at Caer Dathyl to visit Math, that Blodeuwedd walking with her maidens in the gardens at twilight heard the sound of a hunting horn. Soon a weary and very handsome nobleman was knocking at her gates. His name was Gronwy,[6] Lord of Penllyn. He told her he had strayed far from his own lands, hunting a stag. 'The most proper thing,' her maidservants whispered, 'would be to invite him to stay the night.'

As Blodeuwedd looked into the eyes of Gronwy, love entered her heart in a way she had never known. Nor could he conceal the love and desire he felt for her. Nor did they postpone their passion, but slept together that same night.

Gronwy meant to depart next day, but he did not and next night, the burden of their talk was how they might remain together always. Gronwy advised her, 'Find out how Lleu may be killed, since his life is certainly guarded by enchantment.'

'How will I do that?' asked Blodeuwedd.

'Pretend concern for his safety,' said Gronwy, as he took his leave. The next night, Lleu returned.

Noticing Blodeuwedd's quietness, Lleu asked after her.

'Husband,' she said, 'I was worrying about your death. You may think me foolish, but I could not bear it if you died before me.'

Lleu said, 'Worry no more, my love. Unless God kills me, I will be very hard to kill.'

Blodeuwedd (blod éh weth)

'Will you explain then to me, my darling, how you could be killed? For my memory in matters of caution is better than yours.'

'Firstly, my lovely one, whoever killed me would have to spend a year working on the spear, working on it only when people were in church on Sunday. Moreover, I cannot be killed indoors or outdoors, on horse or on foot.'

'Well that's a relief, my dearest. I don't see how you could be killed at all then.'

'Only if a bath were made for me, upon the bank of a river, with a roof frame above it as a shelter, and if a male goat were stood beside the tub, and if I stood one foot on the goat's back, one foot on the bath's rim—whoever wounded me in that position would kill me.'

This was the information Blodeuwedd sent secretly to Gronwy, and he began working on the spear. One year later that spear was finished. Blodeuwedd, with her blandishments, persuaded Lleu to stand in this unlikely position. Gronwy cast the spear at him, striking him in such a way that the shaft broke off but the head remained in his guts. With a terrible scream, Lleu spread wings and flew away in the shape of an eagle.

Gronwy took possession of the court, and added Lleu's lands to his own.

News of this reached Math and Gwydion. Gwydion vowed he would seek Lleu until he found him. He scoured the northern wilds, hill and dale without success, till at last one evening when chatting with a swineherd he learned the man's sow strayed mysteriously each day. Gwydion determined to follow her.

He found that the sow was going each day to a tree to feed on rotten flesh and maggots that littered the ground beneath it. Gwydion know Lleu must be in that tree, and he addressed his foster son in these magic verses, as the bards relate:

oak that grows between two lakes
you darken the air, you shade the valley
but unless I lie, these fallen leaves
are the scattered flesh of Lleu

oak that grows on the high slopes
rain has not rotted you, nor fire consumed
crest of your pride is Lleu Llaw Gyffes
man of a score of strengths to live

oak that grows beneath the crag
refuge of a noble prince
unless I lie, Lleu will come down
out of your arms into mine

Lleu fluttered down from the tree. Gwydion struck
him with his enchanter's staff and changed him back into
his own shape. And a pitiful semblance of a man he looked,
nothing but skin and bones, the ghastly wound of Gronwy's
spear-cast gaping in his side.

Gwydion carried him back to Caer Dathyl, and there
with all their arts, they were a year in healing him. Then
Lleu, in his full strength, besought Math to permit him to
muster an army to march against Gronwy.

But Gronwy had fled to Penllyn, leaving Blodeuwedd
to face the soldiers of Lleu and Gwydion herself alone. And
alone she was, for hearing this army approach, she and her
maidens tried to escape across the Cynfal River. And in
their fear, ever gazing over their shoulders to see who
followed, all were drowned but she.

When Gwydion came to where Blodeuwedd was, he
said to her quite quietly, 'I will not kill you, but I will do
worse. I will let you go in the form of a bird. And because
of the harm you did to Lleu, you shall shun the light of
day, for fear of other birds.' And Gwydion struck her
with his enchanter's staff, and she became an owl. And the
owl is still called Blodeuwedd in Welsh to this day.

From Penllyn, Gronwy sent messengers offering land or gold, as recompense. But Lleu sent word back saying, 'The least I will accept is that he will go to the place where he threw the spear at me and there let me throw a spear at him.'

Gronwy asked his noblemen and his foster brothers if any would take the blow on his behalf, but none would take it. Gronwy came to the shore of the Cynfal River. He stood where Lleu Llaw Gyffes had stood. And Gronwy said to Lleu, 'Lord, since I harmed you under the influence of a woman, let me place that boulder I see between me and your spear-cast.'

'I will not refuse you that,' said Lleu.

'God reward you,' said Gronwy.

He hastened to raise the boulder between himself and Lleu. As tall as himself it was. Lleu took careful aim and cast the spear at him. It pierced the stone and Gronwy also. The spear of Lleu broke Gronwy's backbone in two pieces. So he died.

The stone is still there, on the banks of the Cynfal River, in North Wales. The hole where Lleu's spear passed through it may be seen to this day.

from original Welsh text,
c. eleventh century

134

Cynfal (kúnvyle)

DEIRDRE OF THE SORROWS

The men of Ulster were drinking, one night of many. it was in the house of Feidhlimidh son of king Conchobhar's story-teller, and Feidhlimidh's wife was serving the men their drink, though she was pregnant and very near her time. The men of Ulster were drinking deep that night. Singing and shouting, these heroes. Showing no signs of retiring. Finally the pregnant woman was for leaving them to it. She was for going to her bed. But as she went, the unborn babe screamed in her womb, with such a scream as could be heard throughout the house and by every roisterer there.

Not a man but leapt to his feet, and all of them with the one enquiry. Feidhlimidh's wife bid them ask Cathbhadh the Druid.

Cathbhadh came, and placed his hand on the woman's stretched and rounded belly, feeling the movement of the child within. And Cathbhadh drew in the breath of prophecy, and spoke these words, as the bards relate:

Cradled in your womb there screams
a woman whose colours are like wheat and sea
a woman who will kindle slaughter
among the chariot-masters of Ulster
she will spark murder in the hearts of kings
in the red west she will be a scythe of reaping.

He said the child should be named *Deirdriu*. And this was the name they gave her at her birth.

'Kill this child now,' was the word among the warriors. But Conchobhar the king gave them denial. 'I will take her,' he said. 'I will raise her as I choose. When she is grown to her full beauty, she will warm my bed.'

None dared oppose him. So it befell. She was raised in a place apart, away from the sight of men. Only her foster family by her, and a female bard called Lebhorcham, whose satires of malice were so fearsome that no one cared to put

---

Feidhlimidh (fethlimith)   Cathbhadh (kathvath)   Deirdriu (derdru)

a law of trespass against her.

One snowy winter morning, Deirdriu's foster father was butchering a calf he had killed for her. Deirdriu, watching a raven that was drinking the calf's blood, said quietly, 'I could love a man whose hair was as black as the raven, whose cheeks were as red as the blood, and whose skin was as white as the snow.'

'Fortune is with you,' whispered Lebhorhcam from behind her. 'Such a man lives, and not far away. Noísiu, he is called, one of the three sons of Uisliu.' Deirdriu vowed in her heart she would find a way to meet him.

One day, Noísiu was singing, by himself alone, as he was walking along the walls of the city. Along the walls of Emain Macha. A melodious singer he was. So were all the sons of Uisliu, good singers and good warriors. Deirdriu came along the wall towards him, sauntering the more as she passed him by. She was the most beautiful woman ever seen.

'A fine heifer,' said Noísiu, smiling. He did not realise who she was.

'A heifer among no bulls,' was the reply she gave him. Noísui began to understand it was to Deirdriu he was talking.

'You have the bull of Ulster,' he said, 'Conchobhar the king.' But he had looked into the eyes of Deirdriu, that were as blue as the distance, and he had fallen in love with her himself.

'I would prefer a young bull,' said Deirdriu.

'Ah, Deirdriu, disaster is in what you speak. Foolish even to jest of it.'

'You spurn me,' said Deirdriu.

'You know it must be so.'

Deirdriu grabbed Noísiu hard by his ears. 'These are the two ears of dishonour and scorn, unless you take me.' This curse and spell she put on him that he could not gainsay her.

He began a magic of his own, a singing he could make

Lebhorcham (lévar kham) Noísiu (noy shu) Uisliu (oosh hi)

that set the warriors of Ulster fighting one against the other. There was a brawling and a breaking of heads. On every side of them, the sound of wounds. Many an axe drank blood. Noísiu's two brothers came to him, Ainnle and Ardan. 'Whatever evil comes of this, you will not be shamed while we are alive.'

The three brothers fled, and Deirdriu with them. They sailed to Scotland and offered themselves as warriors to the king there. And because of the beauty of Deirdriu, that put desire on every man that saw her, they kept her hidden as best they could.[1] They feared that death would follow her.

But in spite of all concealment, word of her beauty reached the king of Scotland, at last, and he too determined to have Deirdriu for his own.

Now Conchobhar sent lying messengers to Noísiu, saying 'Oh sons of Uisliu, flower of my warriors, return to Ulster and we will call the past the past.'

But when they returned, Noísiu, Deirdriu, Ainnle and Ardan, they were surrounded by an army led by Éoghan the right hand of Conchobhar. The greeting Éoghan gave to Noísiu was the point of a spear. The spear broke Noísiu's back. The sons of Uisliu met their death on that green shore.

Deirdriu was taken to Conchobhar. In the year that followed she neither laughed nor smiled, nor ever lifted her head from her knee. Whenever musicians were brought to her she would repeat these words, as the bards relate:

'Sweet is your music but I have heard sweeter
sweeter than water was Noísiu's voice
what reason have I to take comfort in music
since Noísiu of the songs is dead'

And whenever Conchobhar would speak to her, she would say:

'wave after wave against the shore
sorrow after sorrows

Eoghan (yowen)

Noísiu I found beautiful
you have put death between us'

'Who do you hate most?' said Conchobhar to her.
'Yourself, and after you, Éoghan.'
'Then you will spend a year with Éoghan,' said
Conchobhar, 'before you return to me.' He took her to
Éoghan. Deirdriu was standing in a chariot between them.
Conchobhar made sport of her, saying, 'Deirdriu, you are a
ewe between two rams.' They were passing a great boulder.
Deirdriu leapt at it so that her skull was smashed.

This story is one of the three sorrowful tales of Ireland.
Cathbhadh the Druid foretold that none of Conchobhar's
line would ever follow him in Emain Macha, and so it
befell. The city crumbled. Wild grass covered it.

from early Irish text
c. ninth century

FIONN MACCUMHAILL AND THE OLD MAN'S HOUSE

MUCH GENTLER AND LESS ANCIENT THAN STORIES SUCH AS Deirdriu are the many legends of Fionn and his heroes— common to Gaelic Scotland and Ireland. Texts of Fionn stories in Ireland date back to the early middle ages. The piece that follows is from the oral heritage of Ireland collected this century.

It is said of the hero Fionn MacCumhaill[1] that if a day goes by without his name being mentioned the world will come to an end. A great hero he was and a man of knowledge. When once he was asked what was the sweetest music in the world he replied, 'The music of what is!' But this is not the story of Fionn I'm telling you.

Fionn was out hunting one time, he was nearly always hunting except when he wasn't hunting. Why wouldn't he love it? His two hounds were his own nephews under enchantment. Their names were Bran and Sceólang. But this is not their story I'm telling.

Fionn had with him this day Conan the Bald who never saw a man frown but he considered it his duty to strike him. Who never saw an open door but he considered it his duty to go through it. But this is not his story.

And Fionn had with him this day Diarmaid of the Love Spot,[2] and he had a certain mark on his face. He had to keep that covered with his hat, because any woman who got a glimpse of it would fall passionately in love with him. And he was one of the finest hunters in the world, though he would never hunt wild boar. But this is not his story either.

This story is of a time they were out hunting on the island of Arran, God bless and keep it forever. But whatever they were hunting they did not catch it but dark of night caught them hungry and far from home.

They stumbled on, and the rain came on. And just as

Fionn MacCumhaill (fiun macool)

they were getting resigned to spending the night in the open, for it was high moors, no trees or caves, not a stick of wood for fire, just the wind whistling up and the rain sluicing down, just as they were getting resigned to this they were fortunate enough, stumbling round a shoulder of granite, to find themselves near a wee cottage. They made their way to the door and knocked. Well, Fionn knocked. Knocked good and loud, too. And in the silence after his thumping, they heard a creaky old voice.

'Time enough, time enough. If I'm to let you in, my fine fellows, you will need to behave yourselves in my house. Och, I'll not stand any shenanigans from you!'

The door creaked open. There stood a wee old man, thin as a reed, and his long, wispy hair, so white, floating round his long white wispy beard and two white brows like brushes on him.

'Och yes, come in. You'll need shelter, I suppose. But,' here he held up a scrawny finger, 'you'll just behave yourselves like gentlemen. Or you'll answer to me.'

Conan looked at Diarmaid and Diarmaid looked at Fionn and Fionn, with a wink to them, answered the old man: 'Thank you very kindly, sir, for your hospitality.' They thought it very strange such a wee spring of a man should talk so sternly to them, but in they came, politely indeed, and sat down by the fire.

There was a young goat frisking about the room. After a wee bit the old man said, 'I wonder if any of you strong lads would be so good as to tether up my wee goat to that ring by the door.'

'I'll do it,' said Conan, and made to take the goat by the collar. But try as he might, he couldn't lay a hold on the goat. She frisked always just out of his reach. Diarmaid tried, and did no better. Fionn tried, and with no more success.

Finally the old man said: 'Och, you fellows are no help at all. I'll need to do it myself. Och yes. If you want a job done you must do it yourself.' And so, grumbling, he hobbled over to the goat, and with no more ado tethered her to the wall.

At this minute a young woman walked in, a radiant beauty, asking them what would they have for their supper, maybe; and not to put too fine a point on it, they were all stricken with love for her. Or something like it. And Diarmaid whom all women loved said to her: 'Bright pulse of my heart, how can I know content without you? Consent to be my own forever . . .' and such words as young men say at these times.

But the young woman rounded on him in anger, saying: 'Once I was yours and little heed you paid me then!' Slamming the door she left the room.

Well, they didn't know what they were to make of this, but at least they weren't out in all the weather. Very little sleep they got, for pure curiosity.

In the morning, when the old man came in, Fionn asked him: 'Sir, why is it that such a frail old man as yourself used such stern language to us, the strongest heroes in the land? And why could you tether the wee goat none of us could catch? And why did the beautiful girl so reply to Diarmaid that once he had possessed her and cared not for her then? For truly neither he nor we have ever seen her before. Who is she at all?'

And the old man said: 'Her name is Youth. Little enough you cared for her when she was yours. The name of the little goat is The World. There's none can bind her but me. And my name is Death.'

THE DIALOGUE OF OSSIAN
AND ST PATRICK

OSSIAN WAS THE SON OF FIONN AND THE GREAT BARD OF
Fionn's warriors. His mother had been transformed into a
deer by a druid called The Dark Man. It was by this deer
that Ossian was raised.

Ossian went to Tír na n-Óg with the beautiful Niamh,
a woman of the Sídh.[1] Of course hundreds of years passed
unnoticed to him while he was there. Returning to Ireland,
he leaned from his saddle to help a man who was trying to
lift a stone. But the girth of Ossian's saddle slipped. He fell
to the earth of Ireland. The weight of his years fell upon
him.

He was taken to meet St Patrick. Now Patrick offered
the aged bard his baptism into the Christian paradise, but,
hearing that Fionn would not be in it, Ossian scornfully
refused, saying, 'Ungenerous is your god.'

'Tell me of this Fionn,' said Patrick.

'Of Fionn's generosity,' said Ossian, 'it is related that
his house was the stranger's home, and if the leaves of the
forests of the world were red gold, and the waters of the
rivers of the world white silver, Fionn would have given
them all away.'

'Without Christ,' said Patrick, 'how were you sustained
in the sadness of life?'

And Ossian replied: 'by honour that was in our hearts,
by strength that was in our arms, by truth that was on our
tongues.'

'Speak to me of something other,' said steel-eyed
Patrick of the many conversions.

'I will speak of Arran,' said Ossian, 'where we would
have the finest hunting that ever we had, for there we
would go from Lammas until the time of the cuckoo.

Plentiful[2] are the stags of Arran
sea-wounded her unshielded shoulder

Niamh (neeav)   Sidth (sheethe)

dale where hungry mouths are filled
hill where steel spears are crimsoned

young deer on Arran's mountains
sweet bramble briars her tangling locks
curling the combing waters of her waters
plentiful the acorns of her oaks

horse hounds and foot hounds in Arran
brambles there as black as sloes
pleasant to live there in shade of trees
plentiful the deer in her oak groves

purple as a king's mantle is Arran's heather
green grass cloaks her rocks
grey scree above her forest hair
where sure hoofed the roedeer skip

flat meads for fat pigs in Arran
a sailing sun for her dappled fields
hazelnuts her hazels crown
high ships with her every tide

sweet Arran in calm weather
under her river banks her trout are lazing
white gulls about her cliffs calling
how sweet is Arran in every season.'

'And I will speak of the craneskin bag that Fionn, my father, had, the bag that once belonged to Manannán MacLir. A treasure bag of many strange powers it was, and this is its story.

Long and long ago, two women fell in love with one man. The man's name was Ilbhreac. And it was Aoife that loved him, Aoife and Iuchra.[3] Now Iuchra had the power of ill-wishing, and she cast on her rival the shape of a crane. But Aoife's human speech was with her still, and with her woman's voice she spoke from the bird beak of her feathered head.

'How long will this curse be on me, beautiful ice-hearted Iuchra?'

Ilbhreac (eelvrek)   Aoife (eefe)   Iuchra (yukhra)

And Iuchra replied: 'Not hard to answer. Two hundred years you will live by the grey waves. Mockery will be your greeting, and no land beneath your feet but the land of Manannán, the endless waters of the sea. And may this curse also be on you, that when you are dead a bag be made out of your skin.'

'So it befell in the full course of time. Manannán Mac Lir took Aoife's skin when she was dead, but for the sake of the woman she had been, he made of it a bag to hold his greatest treasures. The bards of Erin know well what treasures were contained in this craneskin bag. The King of Scotland's shears were in it, the King of Lochlainn's helmet, and the bones of Asail's swine. A belt made of the skin of the great whale was in the bag, and when the tide was full the bag was full, and when the tide ebbed, the bag was empty.

'After Manannán, the bag was in the keeping of Lugh of the Long Arm, till he was killed by the three sons of Cearmaid Honeymouth. They kept it till they were killed by the sons of Míl. And Manannán returned, the Son of the Sea, deathless and unwearied, and carried off the bag again. And how Fionn got it I will at this time instruct you.'

'Speak to me of something other,' said Patrick.

from the original twelfth-century Irish text,
Acallam Na Senørach (Dialogue of the Ancient Men)

NOTES TO PART I

THE WOOING OF ISOLDE

1. March son of Merichion (máre khion) 'horse son of horsing', is the Welsh counterpart of Irish kings Lorc and Labraid and of the Greek King Midas, all of whom are said to have horses' or asses' ears. The legend in Wales is that King March used to kill every man who shaved his beard, in order to keep the secret of his own disfigurement. But on the spot where he buried the bodies of his victims, reeds grew, and any instrument made from them would play only 'King March has horse's ears'.

   For the Celts the horse was symbolic of the powers of fertility. In one Irish tribe a mare was sacrificed, and its blood used for bathing in by the king-elect in a ritual union with the animal.

KING BRAN

1. Bran son of Febal (Fay vil) was a legendary king of Ulster.

2. The Birds of Melody were three magical birds in British mythology associated with the goddess Rhiannon. Their names were Adar Lanach, Adar Lonach and Adar Fwynach; the first sang of love and war, the second of coolness for all aching and the third of the passing of the heart from bondage.

GOGMAGOG

1. Albion was a son of Poseidon and Amphitrite, Lord and Queen of the Sea. He is said to have introduced astrology and ship-building into Britain.

2. Brutus' stone is still to be seen in Totnes in Devonshire, and is said to be the stone on which he first set foot upon landing in Britain.

3. Gogmagog, probably a deity of some ancient and pre-Celtic people, is also mentioned in the Bible by Ezekiel and St John. Recent excavations in the Gogmagog Hills near Cambridge revealed ancient hill figures cut in the turf ... is there some connection with the hill figure of the giant with club at Cerne Abbas in Dorset? Cut in the chalk and connected with fertility ceremonies, this huge phallic figure may originally have been horned. The name 'Cerne' suggests Cernunnos, the Gaulish horned god and Lord of the Animals.

4. 'Maiden Castle' is a term meaning a fortress undefeated in siege, and an early medieval name of Edinburgh Castle is Castrum Puellarum.

5. Lludd (thleethe) was a legendary ancient king of Britain. See his story below, 'The Three Plagues of Britain'.

6. Creiddylad (cray thúl ad) was a spring or virgin deity whose Gaelic form would be Bride, Christianised as St Bridget, the 'Mary' of the Gael.

7. Nudd (neethe) was Nodons, a British deity.

8. Gwythyr ap Greidawl (gwi theer ap grý dowel) was a solar deity, deity of fire, or perhaps a smith deity.

9. The contest between winter and summer for the flowery and fertile earth is represented by the combat between Gwyn ap Nudd and Gwythyr ap Greidawl for Creidyladd every May-day.

CULHWCH AND OLWEN

1. Goleuddydd (gol éy thith) 'bright day' was the daughter of Amlawdd the Ruler.

2. The first to cut a person's hair was considered a kind of god-parent.

3. The Accursed Ridge was Sescenn Úairbeóil in Leinster.

4. Glewlwyd (gleh loid) 'mighty grasp'.

5. Ynyrs (in eers), 'honorius' in Latin.

6. Llychlyn (thlúch lin), 'Lochlann' in Gaelic, Scandinavia.

7. Gleis (glayce) 'stream' . . . Merin 'sea'.

8. Gwenhwyfar (gwen hóy var), Guinevere.

9. Cei (kay) was the Sir Kay of Arthurian Romance.

10. Bedwyr (bédwir) son of Pedrawd.

11. Drych (drukh) 'mirror' . . . Cibddar (kibthar) was one of the Three Enchanters of the Island of Britain.

12. Gwalchmai 'Hawk of May' son of Gwyar was among Arthur's finest warriors, on horse or foot; he was Arthur's sister's son and his first cousin; he later is found as the Sir Gawain of Arthurian Romance.

13. Menw (ménoo), teacher of all knowledge, as he saw written on three twigs growing from the grave of Einigan Gawr.

14. Included among the *anoetheu* or 'difficult things' which Culhwch had to seek and find was the food-producing hamper of Gwyddno Long-Shank — if food for one was put in it a hundred might be fed — one of The Thirteen Treasures of the Island of Britain (listed in The Welsh Triads and written down from the mid fifteenth century)

15. Mabon son of Modron 'Great Son of Great Mother' derives his name from that of a Celtic deity, *Mapŏnos* son of *Mătrona* 'the youth (god) son of the mother (goddess)'

THE MADNESS OF SUIBHNE

1. Suibhne (súvni), Sweeney, prince of North-east Ulster, said to have gone mad in a battle in 637 AD.

2. 'Mo ched-sa fri ced an Choimdedh chumachdaigh,' ar sae 'amail táinicsiomh dom dhíochur-sa agus é lomnocht, gurab amhlaidh sin bhías do ghrés lomnocht ar faoinnel agus ar folúamhain sechnóin an domhain, gurab bás do rinn nosbéra. Mo mallacht-sa for Suibhne bheós agus mo bhennact for Eorainn . . .'
   (Buile Shuibhne, Irish Texts Society, 1913)

3. Uair as amlaidh atá Glenn mBolcáin agus ceithre doirsi ag an ngaoith ann agus roschoill roáluinn rocháoin ann bheós agus tiobrada táobhghlana agus uarána ionnfhuara agus glaisi gainmidhe glanuisgidhe agus biorar barrghlas agus fothlocht fann foda for a lár. Iomda fhós a shamha agus a shiomsáin agus a lus-bían agus a biorragáin, a chaora agus a chreamh, a mhelle agus a miodhbhun agus áirnidhe dubha agus a dercain donna.
   (Buile Shuibhne, Irish Texts Society, 1913)

147

THE SPOILS OF ANNWN

1. In Annwn (anoon) were kept the Sweet Wells of Water and the Perfect Chair of the Bards, as well as the Cauldron, the source and well of poetic inspiration. Annwn seems to be regarded in this poem as an island, or a series of island fortresses. Many of the islands along the west of Britain and Ireland were respected as islands of the dead, as sacred. Gaulish druids looked upon the whole of Britain as an island of the dead, of spirits, certainly as sacred.

2. Gwair son of Geirioedd is mentioned in the Triads as one of the Three Exalted Prisoners of the Island of Britain. The Isle of Wight or Lundy Island may have been the place of his imprisonment.

3. Caer Sidi (kye er sithee) was sometimes used as a general name for all the fortresses; and certainly includes Caer Pedryfan, the Four-Cornered Castle in the Island of the Strong Door, a place of eternal wine drinking, where the grey dusk mingles with a gloom spangled with the yellow flame of torches. Caer Sidi was also called the Invisible Kingdom and the Green Isle.

4. Lleminawg (hlem ín og), cf. *llyminawc* 'the fated one'.

5. Caer Vendiwid (kyre vendée wid) 'fortress of the perfect, a castle of revels like Caer Pedryfan.'

6. The Glass Castle, Caer Wydr or Inis Gutrin, may refer to Glastonbury, traditionally thought of as the physical site of the mysterious Isle of Avalon where Arthur's soul awaits reincarnation. It appears in folk tales as the mountain of glass.

7. Caer Golur may mean Gloomy Castle.

8. The religious myth of Cwy (coy), like that of Gwair and the original myth of Arthur is lost.

9. This ox was one of the Three Prominent Oxen of the Island of Britain, *A'r Ych Brych* 'the Speckled Ox', mentioned in the Triads.

10. Caer Vandwy (van doy) say some means the Castle on High.

11. Caer Ochren may mean Castle of the Slope.

NOTES TO PART II

THE THREE PLAGUES

148

1. Llud (hleethe) son of Beli Mawr 'Great Bel', the Gaulish god Belenus; the Celtic celebration of May, *Beltine* or 'Bel's Fire', may be connected in name with him.

2. The ability of the Corannieid (ko rán yied) to hear any words carried by the air was also an attribute of Math the wizard in the story of Lleu below.

3. The shout of power, with magic to harm or kill, figures in various cultures of the world, among the Aborigines of Australia for instance. The hero Culhwch had this power in his story.

4. This music which brings sleep is mentioned in the story of King Bran. Harpers appear to have played music to soothe, even to heal wounds. The three strings of music traditionally so called were: *geantraige*—music to bring to mirth and joy; *goltraige*—music of honour, valour and tears; *suantraige*—music of repose. And sleep-music is a constant feature of supernatural birds in the Celtic world (see the note to Aoife in Ossian's story at the end of this book).

VORTIGERN'S TOWER

1. Vortigern is mentioned in The Welsh Triads as one of the three disgraceful drunkards of Britain, who, in his cups, gave the Isle of Thanet to Horsa King of the Saxons that he might sleep with Horsa's daughter Rowena. He also gave a claim to the crown of Britain to the son of this union.

2. Apuleius was a Roman author who lived shortly after the time of Christ.

3. The Arthurian wizard Merlin is a composite figure founded upon the fifth-century Celtic bard and pupil of Taliesin, Myrddin ap Morfyrn, whose legendary grave is at Drumelzier in the Borders of Scotland. Myrddin was also the name of an earlier Celtic deity and one of the earliest names for Britain (given in the Welsh triads), *Clas Merdin*, the Enclosure of Myrddin. Among the Celtic legends associated with Merlin, reference is to be found to his Ship of Glass which sails round Britain and which can be seen (if standing upon the right turf and upon the right day) from St David's Cathedral in West Wales. Merlin is said to have carried for safekeeping to Bardsey Island off North Wales The Thirteen Treasures of Britain: these included the veil of King Arthur—whoever looked from under it no one would know him; the basket of Gwyddno (see note to Culhwch above), and the horn of Bran the Niggard from the North—any drink wished for appeared in it.

4. The red dragon and the white were concealed in the story of The Three Plagues of Britain, and are here revealed by Merlin. The red dragon is still the symbol, and flag, of Wales.

5. Aurelianus Ambrosius, second son of Constantine II.

ARTHUR THE EARLY LEGEND
1. Eoppa was a treacherous Saxon.

THE STORY OF THE GODODDIN
1. Aneirin (a nŷ rin) was a North-British (Welsh) poet of the later sixth century.

2. Mynyddawg (minná thawg) was king of the Gododdin (go dóthin) c. 600 A.D.

3. Aeron was probably Ayrshire.

4. Cynon (kúh non) was an Edinburgh man living in Aeron.

5. Nothing is known of their heroes: Caradawg and Madawg, Pyll (pulh) and Ieuan (yie an), Gwgawn (gù gaun) and Gwiawn, Gwynn and Cynfan (kùnvan) and Gwawrddur (gwartheer) and Aeddan.

6. Peredur (pere deer) was a knight who later appears in the Arthurian tales as Sir Percival (Parsifal), as one who achieves a vision of the Grail. Parsifal is a medieval form of the Amadán Mór, the Great Fool who features in early Gaelic material and in folk tales as the simpleton who succeeds in the most extraordinary quests where stronger or less courteous have failed.

MICHAEL SCOT

1. Avicenna was a twelfth-century Arabic scholar and author of nearly one hundred books on medicine, astronomy, theology and poetry. Averroes was also called Ibn Rashid, a twelfth-century Arabian philosopher and authority on Aristotle. Aristotle was the fourth-century BC Greek philosopher whose works, carried by scholars to Arabia after the sack of Rome by barbarians in the early Christian era and preserved in Arabic when other Latin and Greek editions were lost, were preserved for European scholars by Michael Scot.

2. Frederick II (1194–1250) was known as 'Stupor Mundi', a wonder of the world, a great patron of the arts and learning.

3. smoor—damp down.

4. What makes you so pale, all my merry men?
   What makes you look so frightened?
   What makes you hang your heads so sadly?

THOMAS THE RHYMER

1. This very ancient tree was still standing within living memory in the nineteenth century. The practice of tying a rag of one's clothing on a thorn tree beside a holy spring for curative or wishing purposes is still prevalent in Britain.

2. A burn is a small river; bogle means 'ghost' or 'spirit'.

3. The Eildons were called 'Trimontium' by the Romans, and it was an important landmark of religious significance to the ancients. Magical events taking place inside hills are a feature of fairy and witch beliefs, particularly in Scotland. Hills in Scotland called 'law' e.g., Berwick Law, Traprain Law, were associated with witches in the seventeenth century, and oaths sworn there were deemed binding because witnessed by the fairies within. Edinburgh tradition retains the story of the Fairy Boy of Leith, who was in the habit of visiting the fairies every Thursday night underneath Calton Hill.

4. The Queen of Elfland is mentioned in various witch trials. In 1597 Andro Man confessed to carnal dealings with the 'Queen of Elphame', who had a 'grip of all craft', who had attended a harvest meeting riding on a white horse; 'she is very pleasant and will be old or young as she pleases.' (She changes because she represents the moon.)

5. The word 'hell' derives from a Saxon deity Hella, whose unpleasant abode was a place for those who had failed to die honourably in battle.

6. The bards, the sacred poets of the Celts, were oracular poets and speakers of prophecy. In order to become so they underwent

various initiations. As late as the thirteenth century, seven hundred years after the last of the Celtic bards in the Borders, Thomas is apparently laying claim to such an initiation and such a power. In early times truth (*fír flatha*) was a magic power of Irish kings; true judgements were given by true princes, and falsehood would bring disaster upon the land.

7. The Rhymer's prophecies are numerous; one of the most famous prophesied the Battle of Bannockburn, one of Scotland's rare total victories over England: 'The burn of breid sall rin fu' reid.' (Bannocks are a kind of bread, and Thomas was thus predicting that the river of bread will run with blood.) In various folk tales Thomas the Rhymer is found to be still living, either under Dumbuck (Dûn a' Bhuic, Buck's Hill, near Dunbarton) or elsewhere in Scotland. He appears occasionally in search of horses of a special kind or colour. A Scottish Gaelic verse predicts, 'When Thomas of power and his horses shall come, days of plundering shall be on the Clyde.'

NOTES TO PART III

THE BIRTH OF TALIESIN

1. Ceridwen (Kerídwen) was originally a Celtic goddess associated with death, the Cauldron of Rebirth, with the sow who eats her young and with magic. Her name connotes a patronage of bards down to this day in Wales.

2. Afagddu (av ág thee), may mean 'carried by dark wings' or 'utter darkness'. His original name is said to have been Morfran, Great Raven or Great Crow.

3. The Cauldron of Inspiration or Rebirth is a symbol of the source of all things, and becomes in later Arthurian stories the Holy Grail. Inspiration itself and soul were summed up together by later bards in the Welsh word 'Awen'.

4. The fact that Taliesin, set afloat like Moses, was caught in a salmon net, was of significance to the Celts because they regarded the salmon as the fish of wisdom. The story of their wisdom is related below in the note to Boann, who is referred to in The Dialogue of the Two Sages.

5. Gwyddno (gwithno) is said to have been the king under whose rule the land now under Cardigan Bay was lost to the sea. A deep sigh is called 'the sigh of Gwyddno'—because of his sorrow at this disaster.

THE BATTLE OF THE TREES

1. Arawn (arown) lord of the other world.

2. Ogam was the script of pre-Christian Ireland. Its invention was attributed to the god Ogma, a deity with affinities to Hercules. One portrayal of Ogma depicts him pulling people along by strings attached from his tongue to their ears. The alphabet was at first used for inscription on upright stones, letters consisting of a system of notches or grooves along an edge. Later in manuscripts it was written horizontally. The alphabet was often used for magical purposes, individual letters as charms and so on.
   Ancient Irish correspondences of trees to the Irish alphabet are quoted by Robert Graves in *The White Goddess*. The names of the letters and their proper trees are as follows:
   > B—beith—the birch
   > L—luis—the rowan
   > N—nion—the ash
   > F—fearn—the alder
   > S—sail—the willow
   > H—uath—the hawthorn
   > D—duir—the oak
   > T—tinne—the holly
   > C—coll—the hazel
   > M—muin—the vine
   > G—gort—the ivy
   > P—bogtha—the dwarf elder
   > R—ruis—the elder
   > A—ailm—the silver fir
   > O—onn—the furze or gorse, in Scotland, whin
   > U—ur—the heather
   > E—eadha—the white poplar
   > I—idho—the yew

3. It may be mentioned along these lines that a series of highly involved riddles or cyphers on star-lore evolved by sages of the East in ancient times has come down to us as the letters of the English alphabet.

4. Blodeuwedd (blod éh weth) 'flower face' was a beautiful woman made for Lleu son of Gwydion to circumvent his mother Arianrhod's curse that he would never marry a human wife. She was made of nine kinds of flowers: see her story in 'Lleu' below.

5. Brân 'raven' was originally a deity of the ancient Celts. There were three main families of deities in Welsh mythology: the family of Pwyll and Pryderi in the South, who obtained swine from Arawn; the family of Brân in mid-Wales, and the family of Gwydion and the sons of Dôn in the North. The child of Brân's sister is called Gwern 'alder'. His story is part of 'Branwen' below. Brân's further association with the alder is given in this same story.

6. Gorchan 'incantation' or 'canon', the fundamental part of song, of Maelderw (myledéroo), camp of the Gododdin. But the exact meaning of the line is unclear. The word 'derw' (oak in old Welsh) is the root of the word 'druid'. Druid veneration for the oak tree as a symbol of deity was mentioned by Caesar and other Romans.

7. Cader Idris 'chair of Idris', a giant. It is a mountain south of Dolgellau.

THE DIALOGUE OF THE TWO SAGES

1. Emhain Macha (évin mákha), the chief fort of the ancient kings of Ulster. It was named after Macha, a woman or goddess of the ancient Irish, forced by a boast of her husband to race against horses. Though pregnant, she won but died in childbirth at the finish. She cursed in her labour the men of Ulster with a weakness akin to the pangs she suffered, which would overtake them at certain times.

2. Bricriu (brick ree oo) an ancient Ulster hero who loved to cause quarrels.

3. Nechtan's wife was Boann, mother of the god Oenghus, by the Daghdae, principal deity of the tribe of deities called the Túatha Dé Dannan. Boann caused the River Boyne to come into existence: in curiosity she tried to approach the Well Shaded by the Nine Hazel Trees of Wisdom; of all living creatures salmon alone had this privilege. The salmon living in the well swallowed the nuts as they dropped from the trees and became wisdom incarnate. As Boann approached the sacred well, the waters overflowed and drove her before them in a mighty flood. She escaped, but the waters continue to flow to this day. The River Boyne is the hall to which Fercheirtne refers.

4. Núadu's epithet *Argetlám* referred to his silver hand; he was a chief hero or deity of the Túatha Dé Danann, Peoples of the Goddess Donu. Núadu is the Gaelic or Irish representative of the tangled and far-spread web of deities found in Britain as Lludd, Gyn ap Nudd, Nodons and others. The silver arm of Nodons may have been the silver waters of the Severn; and this god was concerned with healing, the sun and water—probably the 'wife' to which Fercheirtne refers.

WEE JACK

1. teetotum—a small four-sided top, originally with a letter on each side, for playing a light gambling game similar to the Jewish dreidel.

2. snell-gabbit—sharp-tongued; cack-handed—clumsy; snibbert—a mean-featured person of no character; slaistery—dribbly; pauchle—a frail, weak and dim person

NOTES TO PART IV

CONALL CROVI

1. Conall Crovi (Konall Krovi) 'yellow-hand', was a story told to J. F. Campbell of Islay by Neill Gillies, a fisherman of Inveraray, April 1856. Several versions of the story are included in Campbell's *Popular Tales of the West Highlands* (I).

BRANWEN

1. Llyr (hleer) was the Welsh form of the Irish sea god Lir.

2. Brân Vendigeit or *Bendigeiwran* 'Brân the Blessed' (later) was grandson of Beli Mawr (see note in 'The Three Plagues of Britain' above). He was a euhemerised deity of the Celts, and Brân 'raven' occurs as an epithet for a warrior in Celtic poetry. The raven is a wise and skilful bird, but also, as a carrion eater, a bird associated with battlefields and the dead. The saying that 'no house can contain Brân' points to his association with the alder, as in ancient times, houses were built on stakes of alder wood over water, for alder is slow to rot. It was not used in houses but under them.

3. Manawydan was the British form of Manannán.

4. Branwen, her name may mean either 'white breast' or 'white raven'.

5. Gwern 'alder'.

6. Rhiannon was a Celtic goddess with an association to the horse and the possessor of three magical birds (see note in 'King Brân'). She was the wife of Pwyll, later married to Manawydan and her name was derived from Rigantona 'great queen'.

LLEU

1. Lleu Llaw Gyffes (hleye hlow guffes) 'fair-haired one with the skilled hand 'was a British form of the young hero-god found in Ireland as Lugh. The main parts of his story take part in Gwynedd (gwineth), North Wales.

2. Pryderi (prid éree) 'anxiety' was the son of Pwyll and Rhiannon. Pwyll (pooilh) 'thought'; his story is Branch One of the *Mabinogion*.

3. Gilfaethwy (gil vye thwee), one of the twelve children of Dôn, who was the British form of the Irish Dana, mother of the gods. Gwydion was chief of the children of Dôn and a powerful magician.

4. Arianrhod 'silver wheel' or 'silver encircled', her fortress has been identified by the bards as the *Corona Borealis* constellation or as the Milky Way.

5. The smallest bird of all, the wren, becomes the King of the Birds in British folktale. The wren is traditionally hunted at mid-winter. In the *Mabinogion*, Gwydion's sister's son Lleu breaks a wren's leg to obtain his name. There is a bardic link between the wren and the hero of the old year, the Christmas Fool—Gwydion. The robin is linked to the young hero of the rising year—Lleu. The youth hero deity traditionally has two aspects, kings of the year, one ruling from May to November and one from November to May— corresponding to the main divisions of the Celtic year.

6. Gronwy (gron oo ee) Lord of Penllyn (pen hlin), on the borders of Bala Lake in North Wales.

DEIRDRE
1. Traditionally, Deirdriu was kept hidden by Loch Etive in Scotland.

FIONN MAC CUMHAILL
1. Fionn Mac Cumhaill (finn macool) 'fair-haired son of Cumhaill' acquired his knowledge and power by eating one of the Salmon of Wisdom ... who had been swimming about the Boyne looking disconsolately for the lost nuts which had fallen from the Hazels of Wisdom into the well Boann had caused to flood centuries earlier. The stories of Fionn and his band of warrior-hunter heroes, the Fenians, are known equally in Ireland and Scotland, and date from the middle of the third century AD.

2. The most famous story of Diarmaid concerns his love affair with Fionn's young wife Gráinne (granya), their elopement and tragic death. Diarmaid was under geasa (a magical *tabu*) never to hunt a particular boar, and Fionn, by causing him to hunt one, engineered his death. While he was pacing its spine to measure it, a bristle pierced Diarmaid's heel and so poisoned him. Ben Loyal in Sutherland is a supposed site of this, a light coloured streak of rock on the north face being called the 'Boar's Scratch'. Megalithic dolmens in Ireland are often said to have been beds of Diarmaid and Gráinne as they fled the wrath of Fionn.

THE DIALOGUE OF OSSIAN AND PATRICK
1. Niamh (neeav) of the Sídh (sheethe), people of the otherworld, the fairy people.

2. This poem on Arran (in the Clyde) was among the most familiar nature poems in Ireland—no less than seven hundred years after it was originally composed, c. 1175:

Árann na n-aghadh n-ioma'
    tadhall fairrge le a formna;

oileán a mbiataí buíonta
   droimne a ndeargtaí gaoi gorma.

Ard os a muir a mullach;
   caomh a luibh, tearc a tonnach;
oileán gorm graíoch gleannach;
   corr bheannach dhoireach dhrongach.

Agha baotha ar a beannaibh,
   mónainn mhaotha 'na mongaibh,
uisce fuar ina haibhnibh,
   meas ar a daraibh donnaibh.

Míolchoin inti is gadhair,
   sméara is airne dhúdhraighin;
dlúth a fraigh lena feáibh
   daimh ar deighil 'm a doiribh.

Díolaim chorcra ar a carraigibh;
   féar gan locht ar a leargaibh;
os a creagaibh caon cumhdaigh,
   surdaíl laogh mbreac ag bíogaigh.

Mín a magh, méith a muca,
   suairc a goirt—scéal is creidte!—
cnó ar bharraibh a fiodhcholl,
   seoladh na sithlong seici.

Aoibhinn dóibh ó thig soineann,
   bric fá bhruachaibh a habhann;
freagraíd faoilinn 'm a fionnall—
   aoibhinn gach inam Árann!

(*Agallamh na Seanóirí*,
Pádraig de Barra, 1984.)

3. Iuchra (yukhra) and Aoife (eefe). Aoife was the sister of Aobh, second wife of Ler, one of the chiefs of the fairies and originally a pagan sea-god. Because of jealousy, Aoife transformed the four children of Ler and Aobh into swans. For nine hundred years they were supernatural swans, retaining human speech and reason, with the gift of making music so beautiful that everyone who heard it fell asleep.

FURTHER READING

Agallamh na Seanóirí, vol. I, ed. Padraig de Barra (Dublin: Foilseacháin Náisiúnta Teoranta, 1984).

Aitken, Hanna—*A Forgotten Heritage: Folktales of Lowland Scotland* (Scottish Academic Press, 1973).

Buile Suibhne, ed. J. G. O'Keeffe (Dublin: The Dublin Institute for Advanced Studies, 1931; reprint of *Irish Texts Society*, XII, 1913).

Campbell, John G.—*Witchcraft and Second Sight in the Scottish Highlands* (Glasgow: James MacLehose and Sons, 1902).

Chambers, Robert—*Popular Rhymes of Scotland* (Edinburgh and London: W. and R. Chambers, 1841).

Dillon, Myles and Nora Chadwick—*The Celtic Realms* (London: Cardinal, 1973).

Early Irish Myths and Sagas, trans. Jeffrey Gantz (London: Penguin Classics, 1981).

Evans-Wentz, W. Y.—*The Fairy Faith in Celtic Countries* (New Jersey: Humanities Press, 1977; reprint of 1911).

Ford, Patrick K.—*The Mabinogi* (University of California Press, 1977).

Geoffrey of Monmouth—*The History of the Kings of Britain*, trans. Lewis Thorpe (Middlesex: Penguin, 1966).

Graves, Robert—*The White Goddess* (London: Faber and Faber, 1948).

Guest, Lady Charlotte—*The Mabinogion* (Chicago: Academy Press, 1978; facsimile reprint of 1877).

Jackson, Kenneth Hurlstone—*A Celtic Miscellany: Translations from the Celtic Literatures* (London: Penguin Books, 1971).

Le Roux and Guyonvarch—*Les Druides* (Rennes: Ogam Celticum, 1978).

Nash, D. W.—*Taliesin; the Bards and Druids of Britain: A Translation of the Remains of the Earliest Welsh Bards and an Examination of the Bardic Mysteries* (London: John Russell Smith, 1858).

O'Cuiv, Brian—*Seven Centuries of Irish Learning, 1000–1700* (Cork: Mercier Press, 1971).

Popular Tales of the West Highlands, vols I–IV, trans. J. F. Campbell (London: Wildwood House, 1984; reprint of 1861–2).

Rees, Alwyn and Brinley—*Celtic Heritage* (London: Thames and Hudson, 1961).

The Triads of Britain, ed. Malcolm Smith (London: Wildwood House, 1977).

Trioedd Ynys Prydein (The Welsh Triads), ed. and trans. Rachel Bromwich (Cardiff: University of Wales Press, 1978).

Thorndyke, Lynn—*Michael Scot* (London and Edinburgh: Thomas Nelson and Sons, 1965).

Welsh Poems, 6th Century to 1600, ed. Gwyn Williams (University of California Press, 1974).